//////// NASCAR

SECR...

...5

by Gina Wilkins

From the opening green flag at Daytona to the final checkered flag at Homestead, the competition will be fierce for the NASCAR Sprint Cup Series championship.

The **Grosso** family practically has engine oil in their veins. For them racing represents not just a way of life but a tradition that goes back to NASCAR's inception. Like all families, they also have a few skeletons to hide. What happens when someone peeks inside the closet becomes a matter that threatens to destroy them.

The **Murphys** have been supporting drivers in the pits for generations, despite a vendetta with the Grossos that's almost as old as NASCAR itself! But the Murphys have their own secrets... and a few indiscretions that could cost them everything.

The **Branches** are newcomers, and some would say upstarts. But as this affluent Texas family is further enmeshed in the world of NASCAR, they become just as embroiled in the intrigues on and off the track.

The **Motor Media Group** are the PR people responsible for the positive public perception of NASCAR's stars. They are the glue that repairs the damage. And more than anything, they feel the brunt of the backlash....

These NASCAR families have secrets to hide, and reputations to protect. This season will test them all.

Dear Reader,

Some people think of writing as a lonely job, involving hours of sitting alone at a computer. Like many writers, I'm a bit of an introvert. I enjoy working at home, close to my family and surrounded by the inhabitants of my imagination. Yet it's always a treat to attend writers' conferences and meet my fellow authors, and I've met some of my closest friends in those gatherings during my career.

I've been a part of several series of connected books, and it's always a joy to work with the other authors involved. Some I've met previously; others become friends through e-mails as we work out all the details. As I'm sure you can imagine, a continuity series of this scope requires a lot of planning and exchange of information, and everyone gets involved, filling our e-mail in-boxes with ideas and suggestions and descriptions. Lively discussions began and warm support was offered when challenges popped up. We all revealed our favorite NASCAR drivers and cheered them on during the season, sharing our love of the sport as we created our own racing families. I hope you have enjoyed the results of that fruitful collaboration.

Gina Wilkins

///// NASCAR®

RISKY MOVES

Gina Wilkins

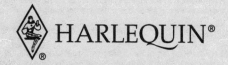

HARLEQUIN®

TORONTO • NEW YORK • LONDON
AMSTERDAM • PARIS • SYDNEY • HAMBURG
STOCKHOLM • ATHENS • TOKYO • MILAN • MADRID
PRAGUE • WARSAW • BUDAPEST • AUCKLAND

ISBN-13: 978-0-373-21796-0
ISBN-10:   0-373-21796-X

RISKY MOVES

GINA WILKINS

A lifelong resident of Arkansas, romance bestselling author Gina Wilkins has written more than eighty books for Harlequin and Silhouette Books. She is a four-time recipient of a Maggie Award for Excellence presented by the Georgia Romance Writers and she was a nominee for a Lifetime Achievement Award from *Romantic Times BOOKreviews*. She credits her successful career in romance to her long, happy marriage and three "extraordinary" offspring.

As always, this is for my family.

REARVIEW MIRROR:

At long last, fugitive embezzler Hilton Branch has been found. He's behind bars, and the Branch family can finally breathe a sigh of relief. Meanwhile, the gossip mill is buzzing about the risk Maximus Racing has taken by firing their established crew chief so late in the season. All eyes are on the new—and inexperienced—crew chief.

CHAPTER ONE

"So, Tobey, how do you feel about replacing the man you claim taught you everything you know about being a crew chief?"

Tobey Harris squirmed a little in his chair, self-conscious in the glare of the bright lights, uncomfortable with the line of questioning introduced by the very attractive woman facing him from a matching chair. "I have nothing but the highest respect for Neil Sanchez. He's a great guy and I wish him success in whatever he chooses to pursue next."

"Can you tell our listeners why he was fired? It had to have been serious for team owner Dawson Ritter to dump the established crew chief this late in the season, with the Chase for the NASCAR Sprint Cup in the balance for your driver, Kent Grosso."

Tobey felt his eyes narrow in irritation. Remembering his onlookers, he tried to keep his emotions out of his voice and expression when he replied, "Neil left the team through mutual agreement, for reasons of his own. As I said, I think he's a great guy. Our team is ready for the upcoming race at Watkins Glen."

His interviewer nodded, making her wavy, shoulder-length chestnut hair sway against the shoulders of the thin white summer sweater she wore with sharply tailored slacks in a muted gray plaid. Her amber-brown eyes were focused intently on his face when she asked the next question. "All right, about the race. It will be the first you've called as a crew chief. How does the rest of the team feel about answering to a young man who was the crew chief's assistant less than a week ago? Especially a baby-faced guy who looks barely older than a teenager himself?"

A few onlookers snickered. Feeling his cheeks warm, Tobey scowled. "Oh, come on—"

"Answer the question, Tobey," a man's voice ordered from the shadows behind the bright lights focused on Tobey's face. "You're going to hear worse."

Sighing loudly, Tobey struggled for patience. This was just a practice interview, he reminded himself. His owner and driver wanted to see how he would conduct himself when hit with the really tough questions. He would prove to them that he could handle whatever was thrown at him—not that he had expected anything quite like this.

"I've served as Neil's assistant for two years, including last year, when our team won the NASCAR Sprint Cup Series championship. I've been active in stock car racing for most of my life, and I've trained for this position for ten years, since I graduated high school. I have received the team's full support during this past week, and I have no doubt that we can take the No. 427 car to Victory Lane next weekend."

"Gonna have to take that chip off your shoulder, son," Dawson Ritter advised, stepping out of the shadows with driver Kent Grosso at his side. "You knew when you took this job that there was going to be talk about your replacing Neil. About your lack of experience as a crew chief. And about that baby face of yours, for that matter. You have to let it slide off your back and not get you riled up."

"I can handle it, sir," Tobey assured his employer. "Doesn't mean I have to like it, though."

With a snort of sympathy, Dawson clapped Tobey's shoulder. "Can't blame you for that. I haven't enjoyed this past week much myself. But we'll all stick together and we'll get through this."

"Yes, sir."

Dawson nodded again, the bright lights reflecting off his balding head. Tall and thin, with piercing blue eyes behind bifocal glasses and prominent ears poking out of his fringe of gray hair, sixty-two-year-old Dawson Ritter had a stern face that belied his kind nature and sharp wit. He intimidated most people upon first meeting. Kent and Tobey had once agreed that Dawson reminded them both of their high school principals, but he was actually one of the nicest men Tobey had ever met.

There was nothing Tobey wanted more than to justify the older man's faith in him. Dawson had taken a risk in promoting an untried crew chief at this point in the season, and Tobey carried that weight with him this week as they approached the next race.

Kent Grosso shifted restlessly on his feet, his dark

hair a mess from running his hands through it, his bright blue eyes shadowed as they had been since the painful decision to fire his friend and former crew chief, Neil Sanchez. Tobey knew how hard that had been for everyone involved. Despite problems with temper and drinking and women, Neil had his likable side, and he'd been a top-notch crew chief until his personal problems had spiraled out of control. Kent, especially, had felt a great deal of loyalty toward the man who'd taken him from rookie driver to NASCAR Sprint Cup Series champion in a relatively short time.

Tobey was all too well aware that Kent was worried about the next race. There was a bond of trust between crew chief, spotter and driver, a rhythm that developed with time and practice. Things had been difficult all season between Neil and the team, but Kent had still known what to expect when he climbed behind the wheel and heard Neil's familiar voice in his helmet. It wasn't going to be easy for the driver to put his full faith in a new crew chief this late in the season.

That so-called practice interview hadn't helped, Tobey thought resentfully as Kent and Dawson moved away, talking in low voices.

He whirled toward the woman who hovered behind him. "Thanks a lot, Amy. You made me look like an idiot in front of Kent and Mr. Ritter. Not to mention the other guys standing around watching."

Amy Barber, Kent's PR representative, had the grace to look just a little rueful, even as she defended her actions. "Dawson told me to be tough with you. You need to be prepared for anything the media asks you—and trust me, I could have been harsher."

It wasn't easy to be angry with Amy. Her wide-set, golden-brown eyes met his gaze evenly, and the expression on her pretty oval face was conciliatory. Not apologetic, exactly—since she believed she had been doing precisely what she was supposed to do—but not confrontational, either. She apparently understood why he was annoyed by the questions she had asked. After all, that had been the purpose for her asking them.

Still…

"That 'baby face' remark was below the belt," he growled, shoving his hands into his pockets. "I'm doing my best to convince Kent that I'm ready to take charge of the team, and you probably undermined any progress I might have made this week."

"I was doing my job," she replied quietly. "And you should get used to it, because you're going to be seeing a great deal of me for the rest of this season."

He felt something tighten in his stomach in response to that…promise? Warning?

Funny to think that he'd spent the past few months occasionally fantasizing about seeing more of Amy Barber.

He supposed this situation proved the old adage. *Be careful what you wish for.*

OKAY, SO MAYBE the baby-face remark *had* been too much. Maybe she could have handled the whole interview a bit more skillfully, Amy thought wearily as she drove toward home later that evening.

She tried to blame the audience for her awkwardness that afternoon. She'd been too aware of Dawson and Kent standing there watching her, judging her effectiveness in getting Tobey ready for the questions with which he would be bombarded all week. A few other team members had hovered in the background, wondering how "the kid" would handle his sudden shove into the spotlight.

But, no, she thought with an uncomfortably candid realization. It hadn't been the audience making her nervous earlier. It had been the interview subject himself.

Tobey Harris. Surfer-boy good looks. Blond-streaked, light brown hair worn touch-temptingly shaggy. Blue eyes framed in ridiculously long lashes. Dimples.

He'd sat in that chair, looking at her with such grave intensity, so different from the blustering, habitually flirtatious older man he had replaced—and Amy's mind had gone blank. She'd actually had to force herself to stay focused on the job, which was hardly characteristic of her.

It wasn't even as if she had just met the guy, she chided herself. She had known Tobey for almost a year, ever since she'd been promoted by Motor Media Group, the public relations company for which she had worked for ten years, to full-time PR representative for Kent Grosso. Yet she had spent very little time alone with Tobey, since he'd tended to stay in the background as Neil's assistant, quietly and efficiently performing his job, doing everything within his power to hold the team together when Neil had started falling apart.

Despite his unassuming manner, Amy had noticed Tobey during the past year. Heck, any woman with a pumping heart and reasonably good vision had to notice Tobey Harris. But she'd kept her attention focused on this job she had worked so hard to obtain, telling herself that she would be a fool to risk her position by flirting with a cute younger man on the team. Between the demands of her job and her family, she didn't have time to flirt, anyway, since there was hardly a spare hour in her schedule if the flirting actually led anywhere.

Now that Tobey had been made crew chief, she was even more relieved that she'd kept that inappropriate attraction to herself. She would have to work quite closely with him and any imprudent actions in the past would have come back to bite her hard in the posterior. So, all in all, it was a good thing she'd resisted when he'd grinned impishly at her from beneath the mistle-toe at the company Christmas party last year, when she'd just started working with Kent during the off-season. And that she'd disentangled herself rather quickly when Tobey had impulsively hugged her after Kent won at Talladega in April.

Tobey had reached for her because she was the closest person to him in the excitement of the win, she had assured herself. He'd have hugged Dawson if the owner had happened to be standing in Amy's spot. But knowing all that hadn't made her heart stop pounding like crazy after the hug, nor had it prevented an uncom-fortable couple of daydreams afterward.

So she had a weakness for pretty surfer-boy types,

she told herself, parking the car in her driveway. She was also a bit too fond of chocolate, happily-ever-after love stories and TV reality shows. She knew when to let herself give in to the occasional indulgence, and when to make use of willpower.

Tobey Harris definitely called for willpower.

Pushing a hand through her work-tousled brown hair, she walked up the steps to the front porch of the small house she shared with her sister and their maternal great-aunt. She was really tired this evening. It had been a hot August afternoon, and she felt rumpled and sticky. Since she was late getting home, as she so often was, Gretchen and Aunt Ellen had probably already eaten, though she knew Aunt Ellen would have kept a plate for her. It would be so nice to have a quiet dinner and crash in front of the TV with a paperback for a few hours….

The minute she stepped into her house, she knew the peaceful evening she'd envisioned was highly unlikely. She could hear Gretchen's raised voice the minute she closed the door behind her. The teary, aggrieved tone let Amy know that her sister was on another rant, and she sighed, aware that this could go on all evening. Heaven save the world from hormonal teenage drama queens, she thought wearily.

Tossing her purse and briefcase onto a table, she moved toward the kitchen.

Aunt Ellen stood in the middle of the room, her back to the doorway, her hands planted firmly on her broad, stretch-pants-covered hips. Gretchen sat at the table, tears streaming dramatically down her round, flushed face, her full lower lip protruding in a pout.

"What now?"

Amy's question made both Aunt Ellen and Gretchen turn in her direction and start speaking at once.

"She won't let me—"

"I told her there's no way—"

"And it's perfectly okay because—"

"I'm sure you'll agree with me that—"

Amy raised both hands and spoke loudly. "One at a time, please. I have no idea what either of you are saying. Aunt Ellen, why don't you tell me?"

"Great," Gretchen muttered. "Hear *her* side first."

Giving her sister a quelling look, Amy nodded toward her great-aunt. "Go on."

"Gretchen wants to go to a sleepover at Brooke's house tonight. I considered letting her do so until I found out that Brooke's parents are out of town—something Gretchen conveniently forgot to tell me. After that, of course, my answer was no."

Amy nodded. "Of course."

"Wait a minute!" Gretchen cried out, jumping to her feet. "At least let me talk before you make up your mind."

"Aunt Ellen has already given you an answer," Amy reminded her sister. "I'm not in the habit of overruling her decisions. Besides, my answer would be the same as hers. You're not having a sleepover at Brooke's house while her parents are out of town."

"But her big sister and brother are there. They're in charge. So, everything will be okay. Please, Amy."

Was there any more painful sound than a fourteen-year-old's high-pitched whine? Amy barely resisted the urge to wince as she replied firmly, "Callie is sixteen and Jacob is barely seventeen. I know them, remember? There's no way I would leave either of them in charge of a sleepover for you and your friends."

"But, Amy—"

"I'm not arguing about this, Gretchen. Brooke and your other friends are welcome to spend the night here, but you're not staying at her house unless her parents are home to supervise."

"That's not fair. Jacob said he would watch out for us—not that we need babysitters. We're fourteen!"

"I said I'm not going to argue with you, Gretchen. Aunt Ellen told you no, and I agree with her."

"But all the other kids are going to be there…"

"That's enough!" Amy didn't like raising her voice to her kid sister, but sometimes it was the only way to make herself heard. "Not another word about this, do you hear?"

Grumbling just beneath her breath, Gretchen flounced out of the room. Amy sighed, knowing the teenager could sulk for hours, which she probably would tonight, if some of her friends really had manipulated their parents into letting them spend the night with Brooke and her notoriously irresponsible older siblings.

She turned to her great-aunt. "How long has that argument been going on?"

"All afternoon, pretty much. Are you hungry? I kept a plate warm for you."

"I'm starving. Thank you."

"You look tired. Sit down and I'll get it for you."

Pouring a glass of cold iced tea from the refrigerator, Amy took a seat at the kitchen table as her aunt slid a plate in front of her and whipped away the aluminum foil that had covered it. "You should have sent her to her room. You don't have to put up with her whining."

"I can handle her." Sitting across the table with a glass of tea for herself, seventy-five-year-old Ellen Berry looked quite capable of handling just about anything. Her lined face was set in a no-nonsense expression, her amber eyes gleamed sharply behind the lenses of her silver-framed glasses and her gray curls had been sprayed to withstand hurricane-strength winds.

Amy knew Aunt Ellen looked sterner than she really was, but she wasn't going to dispute the older woman's ability to handle a sullen fourteen-year-old. Still, she worried. As both Ellen and Amy grew older, the problems increased. At thirty-one, Amy was trapped solidly between her teenage sister and senior-citizen great-aunt.

Which, she reminded herself, was only another reason why she had no time for romantic liaisons, either in or out of the workplace. As her sister's legal guardian and the only means of support for their household other than Aunt Ellen's pension, she had enough on her plate as it was.

And speaking of which…

"This pork loin is delicious, Aunt Ellen. You made it a bit differently than usual, didn't you?"

"I used a recipe I found in one of my magazines this month. I thought it turned out well."

"Very well. The potatoes and carrots are good, too. But then, I'm starving," Amy admitted with a slight laugh. "As good as this meal is, I have to admit that just about anything would taste good tonight."

Aunt Ellen shook her head in displeasure. "You skipped lunch again, didn't you?"

"I ate lunch. I think."

"Yeah? What did you have?"

Trying to remember, Amy stabbed her fork into a tender new potato. "I'm sure I must have had something," she muttered, though she was much less positive now.

It had been a hectic day, she thought rather grumpily. Her phone hadn't stopped ringing, and someone had been trying to get her attention nearly every minute. She suspected her voice mail was filling up even then, but she'd silenced her cell phone while she ate, since Aunt Ellen disapproved of telephone calls at the dinner table.

Still shaking her head, her great-aunt grumbled, "You're going to make yourself sick is what you're going to do. Working fourteen hours a day, six days a week, and usually another couple of hours on your one day off. Holding that phone to your ear and trying to hear over the noise of the race tracks…it's a wonder you don't go deaf. Skipping meals, not getting enough sleep, all the stress of the team upheaval you've been dealing with the past few months. I can't imagine why you want to put yourself through that when you could easily get a less demanding job."

It was a conversation they'd been having with increasing frequency for the past eight months, ever since

Amy had been promoted to full-time public relations representative for reigning NASCAR Sprint Cup Series champion Kent Grosso. Amy was aware that she tended to be a workaholic. A lifelong overachiever, she gave everything she had to her responsibilities, whether to her family or her job. That tendency had only grown stronger when she'd become responsible for her much-younger sister ten years ago.

"I love my job, Aunt Ellen," she said patiently, as she did every time the subject arose. "I've worked very hard to get here. I'm so grateful to Sandra for promoting me. As for the challenges the team is facing this year, well, that's what my job's all about, really. Putting the best spin on even the most difficult situations my driver faces. It keeps me on my toes."

"And you love that," her aunt conceded with a light sigh. "So, how did it go with that new crew chief today? Tobey, right? The one you said looks so young he has to show an ID just about every time he orders a beer."

Amy winced. "Apparently he's very sensitive about his youthful appearance."

"Well, that makes sense, I guess. He's in charge now. He needs to convey an air of authority."

"That's pretty much what he said. And I do under-stand. But he has to realize that people are going to notice, and there's always someone who'll think it's funny to comment."

Hearing something in Amy's voice, Ellen cocked her head. "Did you and Tobey have words?"

"Not exactly. He just didn't like the way I prepped

him for the tough interviews he faces this week." Though she had only been doing what she'd been instructed to do, she reminded herself defensively. It had just been easier for Tobey to take out his frustration on her rather than the owner or driver.

"You should invite him over to dinner sometime," Aunt Ellen suggested. "You'll be working so closely with him, you should try to make friends."

"Tobey and I have always been friendly enough. We just haven't spent a lot of time together, since I've worked primarily with Kent and Neil. It'll take a little while for everyone to adapt to the new pecking order, but we don't have a lot of time with the season already more than halfway over. Tobey has only four races to make sure Kent stays in the Chase, so every day is crucial during these next four and a half weeks. At least we had last weekend off, so everyone had a little more time to adjust."

"I didn't notice *you* having any extra time during the off weekend."

"I had to handle the press releases about Neil's departure. It was…difficult." She picked up her now-empty dinner plate. "Which is why I have to get back to work tonight. I have a lot of e-mails to read and reply to and a couple more calls to make this evening. Gretchen will probably sulk in her room for an hour or so, which should give me time to get through most of what I have to do. I'll talk to her after that, once she's calmed down."

"You've got too much on your shoulders," Aunt Ellen

muttered. "When someone tries to take on too much, something is bound to go wrong."

Amy hoped her aunt's pessimism wasn't an omen for the rest of this tumultuous racing season.

CHAPTER TWO

TOBEY HAD JUST completed a meeting with the fab shop crew early Tuesday morning when his cell phone vibrated against his hip. He glanced down at the readout, saw that it was Amy and lifted the phone to his ear even as he walked into the office that was now his. The cluttered room still smelled faintly of coffee, booze and cologne, a mixture that evoked memories of the former crew chief. "Harris."

"Tobey, hi, it's Amy," she said unnecessarily. "How's it going so far today?"

The latest team meeting had been more tense than he had expected. It wasn't as if he was a stranger to the guys. Team insiders were aware that he'd been covering for Neil for several months, trying to hide the fact that Neil had been falling apart, hoping against hope that his old boss would somehow get himself back together. Still, Neil had been in charge even then, making final decisions, sometimes choosing the opposite of what Tobey advised just to prove he was still in charge, which hadn't helped his case when Dawson had finally had enough.

Tobey's management style was going to be very different from Neil's, and he figured he might as well make that clear from the start. While he considered himself a friendly sort, hardly an iron-fist dictator, when it came to getting his team to the top he didn't see any need to fool around. Neil had been good at what he did—until the last few months, anyway—but much less hands-on in some areas than Tobey would be.

Some of the guys weren't going to like the changes; others would prefer Tobey's more detail-oriented and less seat-of-the-pants way of operating. During the next couple of days, he'd find out which ones were willing to make the switch.

It was barely 9:00 a.m., and he'd been at work for four hours. He'd already popped two ibuprofen and a couple of antacids—and he'd been a crew chief for just over a week. He was going to have to chill out, he told himself, or he would develop an ulcer before he called his first race. "It's going okay. What can I do for you, Amy?"

"I just wanted to remind you about the student tour this afternoon at three. You'll need to meet us in the reception area."

"Student tour?" he repeated blankly.

"You looked at Neil's calendar, didn't you? This event has been scheduled for months. It's part of a summer program for gifted and talented teenagers who are interested in racing-related careers like engineering. This is their big, end-of-the-session field trip, a chance to tour Maximus Motorsports HQ with Kent's crew chief. It's our fourth year to participate, something that was started by my predecessor, and which Neil always supported."

"Oh, man, Amy, this is a terrible time for me. I've got half a dozen more meetings today, and about a million other details to attend to. Can't you get someone else to take the kids on the tour? It's not really a crew chief's usual duty."

"No, it isn't. Which is what makes this a special reward for the kids, the chance to meet a real crew chief. You don't have to spend as much time with them as Neil did, but you should give them ten or fifteen minutes to ask you some questions and pose for pictures. Kent's going to make a brief appearance, and there will probably be some press coverage. It would look bad if you skipped out on something Neil always managed to work in."

He grimaced. Already he was getting tired of the "but Neil always did it this way" argument. Neil was gone, and everyone was going to have to get used to that. But because this commitment involved teenagers and Tobey hated disappointing kids, he sighed and said, "I'll be there."

"Great. Three o'clock."

"Three o'clock," he repeated, making a mental note. "And later, you and I need to sit down and discuss anything else you had scheduled for Neil that I should know about."

"Absolutely. We should have done that already, but we've both been so busy putting out fires for the past week that there hasn't been a chance yet."

Someone was standing in the doorway of Tobey's new office, trying to get his attention. It looked as if there might be a line forming out there. "Fine. Gotta go. See you this afternoon."

He clicked off the phone before she had a chance to respond.

Amy scowled at her phone. "He hung up on me," she muttered.

"Were you talking to Tobey? Because he's looking pretty stressed."

Glancing around, Amy saw Kent leaning against the doorjamb to her office, a thick file in his hands. "Yes, it was Tobey. I just reminded him about the student tour this afternoon. He's snowed under, but he promised to fulfill the obligation Neil made. You haven't forgotten that you said you'd drop by, have you?"

"No, it's on my schedule. I can only stay a few minutes, but I'll be there."

"Good. I'm pretty sure a reporter for *Track Talk* magazine is going to be there. We'll get a couple of shots of you and Tobey looking chummy and comfy with each other and being nice to the kids."

Kent nodded, his handsome face grave. "I'll do my part."

"Remember, Kent, it's very important that you express the utmost confidence in Tobey's leadership skills. You regret what happened with Neil, but you're convinced that you and Tobey can win races together. Yada, yada, yada."

He made a face. "I know what to say, Amy. You've

had me spinning this situation ever since we let Neil go. I've been spinning so much I'm getting dizzy."

She gave him a faintly apologetic smile. "Sorry. I'm sure you know what to do. My inner control freak just slips out every once in a while."

"Which is why you're in this job." He tossed the file on her desk. "The signed photos you asked for. I'm going down to the shop. I'll see you this afternoon."

She reached for her ringing telephone. "Thanks, Kent."

Even as she answered her call, she reached for the half-finished roll of antacids in her desk drawer.

AT TEN AFTER three, Amy found herself facing fifteen eager teenagers and three somewhat frazzled chaperones in the lobby of Maximus Motorsports headquarters. Tobey was nowhere to be seen, nor was he answering his cell phone. She had already welcomed everyone, introduced herself and explained what they would be seeing during the tour—and now she was at a loss.

Aware of the magazine reporter hovering nearby, wondering what was going on with the new crew chief, she asked, "So, are there any questions?"

A red-haired boy with prominent ears and a smattering of freckles across his nose raised a hand. "I thought we were going to meet Kent and his crew chief, Neil Sanchez?"

A girl with her brownish-blond hair pulled into a low ponytail sighed heavily. "Don't you keep up at all, Andy? Neil Sanchez is out. Tobey Harris is in."

Andy flushed. "I forgot. Besides, I'm a Justin Murphy fan, remember?"

"Andy, don't be ungracious," one of the chaperones murmured, glancing nervously at the reporter. "Today we're all Kent Grosso fans, since his team is being so kind to host us."

"So where's Kent? Where's the crew chief?" another boy asked.

Amy shifted on her feet and cleared her throat, wishing she had an answer. "Kent will be here in a bit. And I guess Tobey's been delayed. He's very busy right now getting ready for this weekend's road race at Watkins Glen. It will be the first race he'll call for Kent, you know, and he has a lot to do to get ready. In the meantime, maybe I can answer a few questions and then we can start our tour."

And if Tobey hadn't shown up by then, she would hope that Kent's appearance—she crossed her fingers behind her back that Kent would remember to show up—would appease the kids. And as soon as the tour was over, she would find Tobey Harris and…

"Why did Neil Sanchez get fired?" yet another boy asked. "I thought he and Kent were tight. They always acted like best buds when I saw them on TV."

"Kent and Neil are still good friends," Amy replied with a bright smile. "They had a great run together, culminating in the NASCAR Sprint Cup Series championship last season. But it was time for a change for both of them. Now, if you'll all move toward the elevators…"

"I'm so sorry I'm late." Tobey arrived in a rush of

apologies, his expression rueful. His blond-streaked hair tumbled in an attractive mess around his face, as he turned a meltingly repentant smile toward the visitors. Amy could almost hear every female in the group sigh in appreciation, even as the boys responded to Tobey's casually friendly manner. The magazine representative, also a young woman, immediately raised her camera.

Tobey shook hands with everyone, repeated names as they were introduced, charmed the girls and joked with the boys, then apologized again to the chaperones. He introduced himself to the magazine writer, promising a telephone interview later in the week. Within minutes he had them all eating out of his hand.

Amy was frankly amazed. This was the rather reticent, stay-in-the-background, even a little shy Tobey she'd thought she knew? She had seen him deal with the press during the past few days, and he'd handled himself well, though he had been a bit more reserved than she would have liked for his first impression on the fans. But with these kids…well, it was no wonder that the girls in the group were already smitten with him.

She was having a hard time looking away from him herself.

Only a few minutes after Tobey's arrival, Kent strolled in, and the excitement in the room intensified. Amy had seen Kent and Tobey side by side many times during the past year, of course, but now she saw them through the eyes of the starstruck teenagers and chaperones and she realized what a striking team they made.

Two young—Kent was only two years older than
Tobey—handsome, virile, stylish men with high-profile
jobs so many people dreamed of doing; who could
blame the visitors for being dazzled?

Kent and Tobey stayed with the group for about
fifteen minutes, answering a barrage of questions, posing
for dozens of pictures, signing autographs and handing
out the gift bags Amy had put together for the group—
T-shirts, caps, mugs and key chains all featuring Kent's
face, car and sponsors. And then Tobey announced with
credible regret that he and Kent had to leave.

"We have to get ready for this weekend's race," he
explained over the protests that ensued. "We leave for
New York Thursday morning, and we have a lot to do
to get ready for qualifying on Friday. We hope you'll all
be watching Sunday afternoon."

"Will you wave to us?" one of the girls asked hope-
fully, the question apparently directed to both men.

The men shared a glance, then Kent replied, "We'll
wave. Like this," he said, giving a two-finger salute.
"When you see us do that, you'll know we're saying
hello just to you guys."

That seemed to please their visitors, who all assured
them they would be watching for the signal. Amy made
a mental note to remind both Kent and Tobey to give
that wave at least once on Sunday when they found
themselves in front of a television camera. That was,
after all, her job as the team's PR rep.

To fill the silence Kent and Tobey's departure left
behind, she launched immediately into her official-tour-

guide mode, directing the group to move toward the elevators. She would spend the next forty-five minutes or so taking them through the museum area downstairs, the shops, a hauler and then finish up in the gift store, where they could buy any officially licensed souvenirs that caught their eyes and wallets. And then she would spend another six hours trying to catch up on the work she missed while she fulfilled this obligation.

IT WAS ALMOST 7:00 p.m. by the time Tobey had an hour free to eat dinner that evening. Just for a break, he decided to leave the Maximus Motorsports compound for that meal, though he knew he'd be returning for another couple of hours that evening. He pushed a hand through his hair as he headed for the parking lot, trying to decide whether he was in the mood for a burger or pasta. His steps faltered a bit when he saw Amy leaving the building at the same time he did.

He cleared his throat as he approached her. "Getting away late tonight, aren't you?"

She shrugged. "I've been here later."

Her voice wasn't exactly cool, but definitely not as warm as usual. He figured she was still ticked off with him about his tardiness earlier. "Um, sorry I was late this afternoon. I got held up longer than I expected in a conference call."

She nodded. "I figured it was something like that. But you made up for it when you showed up. The kids really enjoyed meeting you and Kent."

"The rest of the tour went well?"

"Oh, sure. No problems."

"Good. Anyway, I guess you're ready to get out of here. I'll see you later, okay?"

"Tobey."

He'd already taken a couple of steps away before she spoke, and something about her tone made him think she'd detained him impulsively. He turned to face her again, thinking that even after a long, hard day at work, she still looked amazingly fresh and pretty. "Yeah?" he asked, distracted by the observation.

"Would you be available to have dinner at my place tomorrow night?"

That question got his attention again, and fast. "Um—dinner? With you?"

She nodded somewhat shortly. "We need to talk about a few things you might encounter in New York. Kent and I are going to have a detailed strategy meeting late tomorrow afternoon, and I figured you and I could talk over dinner, if that's convenient. After all, we both have to eat, so we won't be taking any extra time away from either of our other obligations. I live pretty close to here, so it wouldn't take any longer than going to a restaurant for a meal. You wouldn't have to stay long if you need to get back to the shop afterward."

He told himself he wasn't disappointed that she hadn't been asking him on a date, as he'd first thought, improbable as the idea had been. But it was pretty hard to ignore the deflated feeling caused by her careful explanation.

"You're right," he said, "I will be pretty busy tomorrow night, getting ready to leave for New York and all."

She nodded. "I understand. It's just that I have a feeling you and I haven't exactly gotten off on the right foot since you were promoted. We're going to be working very closely together, so it's important that we get along for the team's sake. Both of us have only one goal in mind this season, of course—making sure Kent wins another championship. Neil almost tore the team apart—it's up to us to put it back together."

Us? She made it sound as though the two of them would be working side by side, equally responsible for getting the car into Victory Lane. He guessed he understood what she was saying. Every member of the team was important, from the offices to the shops to the pits. He, Amy and Steve Grosso, Kent's cousin and spotter, were probably the three who spent the most one-on-one time with Kent, though rarely all of them at the same time.

He doubted that she'd ever invited Neil to her place for dinner. But then, she and Neil had never seemed to have to work very hard at getting along. Neil had occasionally gotten impatient with all the public relations hoops Amy put him through, but she was one of the few people Tobey had never heard Neil raise his voice to. Of course, she'd never called Neil "baby-faced" in front of everyone, either.

"I could probably spare an hour or so for dinner," he conceded.

He couldn't really tell from her expression whether she was pleased that he'd accepted the invitation, but she seemed satisfied with the arrangement. And while he still questioned the necessity for the dinner meeting, he supposed it couldn't hurt to stay on the PR rep's good side. After all, he would depend on her to present him in his best light for the remainder of the season. It would help if *she* also had a good opinion of him. The afternoon's tardiness, despite being due to reasons out of his control, certainly hadn't advanced his cause with her.

ANOTHER TRYING DAY, Amy thought wearily the next afternoon. It had started off with the release of a sports magazine's interview with Neil Sanchez, who came across both bitter and aggrieved that he'd been replaced in midseason as Kent's crew chief. Neil made it sound as though the firing had come as a complete surprise to him, basically through no fault of his own.

He'd painted Dawson Ritter as a distant, coldly competitive owner to whom nothing mattered but the bottom line, and Kent as a man who had let his ambition and hunger for another championship take precedence over his gratitude to the people who'd gotten him where he was. Neil had even had the audacity to make a veiled reference to a scandal earlier in the season, when Kent had openly admitted to being expelled from State University for cheating on a major test. In an unconscionable betrayal of their years of friendship, Neil had implied that the juvenile failing had been a hint of character flaws to be revealed later.

As for Tobey, Neil had portrayed him as a scheming rookie who'd manipulated himself into the crew chief position despite his lack of maturity and experience. One would think from what he'd said that Tobey had been involved in Neil's firing, an implication that was both inaccurate and unfair.

Kent had been infuriated by the things Neil said, and it was all Amy could do to convince him not to over-react. Instead, they released a carefully worded statement expressing gracious disappointment with Neil's comments and sincere best wishes for the former crew chief's future endeavors. It had taken her three hours and four meetings to craft that two-paragraph release to everyone's satisfaction.

She'd spent the remainder of the day fielding interview requests for Kent and Tobey, and reassuring sponsor reps that the negative publicity would quickly die down, especially when Kent and Tobey proved that they were still very much in the running for the current championship. Kent was respected throughout the racing community as a decent, honorable man, she had reminded them all. Neil's personal problems had been equally well known, if previously discussed only in grim whispers. It would do no good for anyone on Kent's team to respond to Neil's accusations with angry retorts, even if they were true. The team would take the high road, and ultimately everyone would benefit from it, she had promised repeatedly.

She arrived home tired and emotionally battered, wishing she could just forget about work for the rest of the evening and vegetate for a few hours. But since Tobey would be joining them for dinner that evening, and he was due to arrive less than twenty minutes after she stumbled through the door, she knew she would be preoccupied with the job for a while yet. After the day they'd had, she doubted that Tobey would be in the mood for inconsequential small talk.

At least her family seemed to be in reasonably good moods, she thought, noting that her great-aunt was humming as she finished dinner preparations and Gretchen was in the den, talking animatedly into the ever-present telephone at her ear. Gretchen gave a little wave when Amy came in, both in greeting and as an implicit signal that she was finally willing to forgive Amy for their disagreement the other night. Not that Amy had asked for forgiveness, of course, still believing absolutely that she'd been right, but such subtleties had never particularly mattered to her younger sister.

"Dinner's almost ready," Aunt Ellen reported with a smile of greeting. "I'll just keep everything simmering until Tobey arrives."

"Thanks, Aunt Ellen. It smells delicious. I'm starving."

"Your favorite," the older woman announced. "Shrimp Creole. I'll serve it over steamed rice with wheat rolls and a small green salad on the side. I made strawberry shortcake for dessert."

Amy's tummy rumbled in response to the menu. "Tobey had better get here soon or there won't be anything left."

Her great-aunt laughed and waved her out of the kitchen. "Go freshen up before your company arrives. I'll stay here and guard the food."

"So who's this guy you're bringing to dinner?" Gretchen asked, tagging along as Amy hurried to her room to change. "Is he cute?"

"Gretchen, he's a co-worker. He's coming to discuss the weekend ahead, not to socialize."

"So why did you ask him to come here instead of joining you at a restaurant like you usually do for your business dinners?"

It was a logical question. Amy wished she had a better answer than having impulsively given in to a suggestion made by their great-aunt. "It just seemed like there would be fewer distractions here," she said somewhat lamely. "I trust you and Aunt Ellen won't interrupt if Tobey and I get involved in a professional discussion."

Gretchen rolled her eyes, which were the same amber-brown as Amy's own. "I'll try to pretend to be invisible. Or I could really be invisible if you'd let me go to Brooke's house for the evening."

"Are Brooke's parents home yet?"

"Not until tomorrow. But—"

"Then you'll have dinner here." Pulling a shirt and pair of slacks from the closet, Amy tossed them on the bed.

Gretchen's expression wavered between irritation and exasperation. Probably assuming the former wouldn't change her sister's answer, she gave in to the latter. "You aren't going to wear that, are you?" she asked, motioning toward the bed.

Glancing at the plain green camp shirt and khaki slacks she'd selected, Amy asked, "Too casual?"

"Too boring. You might as well just go get something out of Aunt Ellen's closet."

"I told you, tonight is strictly business. I've had a long day. I'd like to be comfortable."

Gretchen spoke from within the depths of the closet. "You can be comfortable without looking frumpy. Here. Wear this."

Looking at the summery, sleeveless top and cropped-pants set Gretchen had tossed at her, Amy shrugged. It was a comfortable outfit, casual enough for the evening, yet a bit more trendy than the clothes she'd selected for herself. "Okay, if it makes you happy, I'll wear this. But I have to hurry. Tobey will be here soon."

"So, hurry," Gretchen replied, heading for the door. "And put on some blush. You could use a little color on your face."

"Thanks a lot," Amy muttered, but her sister was already gone. Glancing in the mirror, she grimaced. Okay, so maybe the trying day had left her a bit pale. She supposed it wouldn't hurt to brush a little blush onto her cheeks. Not that she was making a particular effort for Tobey's sake, she assured herself. It was just that he would probably take her more seriously if she didn't look completely stressed out.

She had just finished primping when Gretchen burst back into the room. "Are you ready? 'Cause I think I just heard a car turn into the driveway."

Moving toward the window that looked out over the front lawn, Gretchen gasped. "That car is sweet. Some sort of red sports car. And there's a guy getting… Oh, wow."

She turned her head to look at Amy with huge eyes. "Is that the new crew chief?"

Glancing out the window, Amy couldn't deny the jolt that hit her at the sight of Tobey with his gold-streaked hair gleaming in the early evening light, his slender physique nicely outlined by a blue team polo shirt and khaki slacks. Obviously he had the same effect on Gretchen as he'd had on the impressionable teenagers from the tour yesterday. She hated admitting that she was still just as susceptible.

"Yes, that's Tobey. You've seen him before, haven't you?"

"When would I have seen him?" Gretchen demanded with a scowl. "You never let me go to the tracks."

It wasn't far from the truth. Amy had taken Gretchen on a couple of off-hour tours of the shop and tracks, but she didn't like to have her family around while she was working. She didn't think it looked professional, and she didn't want to be distracted on the job. She'd had this position for less than a year, and she wanted to get off on the right foot. She liked the job, it paid well enough to support her little family, and despite the long hours and extensive travel, she wanted to remain Kent's PR rep for the foreseeable future.

She moved toward the doorway. "Well, come on. You can meet him now. I think you'll like him."

"I can almost guarantee it," Gretchen murmured, following closely behind her as the doorbell rang downstairs.

CHAPTER THREE

TOBEY LOOKED AT the house in front of him and then double-checked the address written on a scrap of paper in his right hand. Yes, this was the right place. He just hadn't expected Amy to live in a tidy, white frame cottage in a neighborhood that looked more suited to retirees and young families than to a single woman in her early thirties.

Tucking the paper into his pocket, he glanced uncertainly at the package in his left hand. He had brought the gift on an impulse that he was now rethinking. He didn't want Amy to get the wrong idea—or to fear that he had misinterpreted her invitation to a simple business dinner. But it seemed too late to take the gift back to his car, so he rang the doorbell, mentally practicing an offhanded presentation of the wine he'd brought with him.

The words left his mind when the door was opened by a somewhat heavyset woman with iron-gray curls and Amy's amber eyes. Obviously a relative—the resemblance was too close to be coincidental.

She smiled. "You must be Tobey. I'm Amy's great-aunt, Ellen Berry. Come on in. The girls will be down in just a minute."

Girls? Tobey had honestly thought this dinner was going to be one-on-one with Amy. How did she intend to talk business if her family was dining with them? "It's nice to meet you, Mrs. Berry."

"It's Miss Berry—I never got around to getting married—but please call me Ellen. Oh, here are the girls. Amy, your guest is here."

"So I see." Looking as fresh as if she hadn't just spent a long, trying day at work, Amy stepped off the stairs with a smile of greeting for Tobey. "I assume you've met my aunt Ellen. This is my sister, Gretchen."

Noting that Amy's sister was quite a few years younger, Tobey gave a friendly nod to the girl. "Nice to meet you, Gretchen. I'm Tobey."

The girl blinked, her youthful face pink when she said with an obvious attempt at sounding older, "It's nice to meet you, too, Tobey. Welcome to our home."

"Thank you," he replied somberly, before turning to Amy, who looked as though she was trying not to roll her eyes. "I wasn't sure what you were serving for dinner, so I brought white wine," he said, holding out the bag he'd carried in. "Since you're being so kind to feed me tonight," he added a bit awkwardly.

Amy accepted the bag graciously, her smile flickering when Gretchen blurted out, "Amy doesn't drink alcohol. Neither does Aunt Ellen."

So much for all his stewing over whether he should bother to pick up a bottle of wine, whether Amy would misinterpret the gesture, whether he should buy the red or the white. "Um…"

"It was very nice of you to bring it," Amy said, giving her sister a look that made the teenager's cheeks darken again. "We'd be happy to open the bottle for you, if you'd like."

Wishing now that he'd never made the stop at the store, he shook his head. "I'll just have what everyone else has."

"Dinner's ready," Ellen said, looking as though she was taking pity on him. "Let's go eat, shall we?"

The other three agreed with almost comic eagerness.

Tobey's relief was short-lived. He looked down in dismay at the dish Ellen set in front of him. Served over fluffy rice, the steaming Creole looked and smelled delicious, thick with tomatoes, onions, spices and plump, pink shrimp. A small green salad and a crusty roll were served as side dishes, with iced tea to drink. He suspected that Ellen had gone to a great deal of trouble over the meal. Considering everything else that had gone wrong between him and Amy so far this week, he was tempted to just eat the Creole. But since he had to leave for New York in the morning, he doubted that he had time for an emergency room visit tonight.

Amy must have read his expression. "What's wrong, Tobey?"

"Oh, dear, I hope you don't dislike Creole," Ellen fretted. "I know there are people who don't like seafood or tomatoes, but I'd already planned to serve this when Amy told me you were joining us. It's her favorite. I should have asked…"

"The dish looks delicious. And I'm sure it tastes even

better," he said ruefully. "The problem is, I'm allergic to shellfish. Seriously allergic."

"And a common allergy that is, too," Ellen responded after a moment, obviously still chiding herself. "I should have had Amy ask you if there was anything you couldn't eat. I'm going to make you something else right now. What would you like?"

"No, please, don't go to any trouble. Your own meal will get cold. I'll just have salad and bread. I'm not really all that hungry, anyway."

"Nonsense. I've never met a young man who wasn't starving by dinnertime. You just eat that salad for a start and I'll have something else for you in a jiffy. Do you like ham-and-cheese omelets?"

"Of course, but I really wish you wouldn't—"

"Too late," Amy told him as her aunt, carrying the offending plate of Creole, bustled out of the dining room toward the kitchen. "She won't be satisfied now until you're too full to move. Aunt Ellen loves nothing more than feeding people."

"I'm allergic to ginger," Gretchen volunteered, as if to make Tobey feel less self-conscious about his weakness. "It makes me puke."

"Gretchen," Amy murmured with a sigh.

"Well, it does. What does shellfish do to you, Tobey?"

He smiled crookedly. "It makes me swell up like a puffer fish and stop breathing."

"Oh." The girl glanced at the innocent-looking shrimp on her plate, then shook her head. "I wish Brussels sprouts would do that to me. Aunt Ellen thinks every growing teenager should eat Brussels sprouts at least once a week, and I hate 'em."

Tobey chuckled and took a bite of his salad. "So do you all live here together?"

Again, it was Gretchen who spoke first. "Yes. Amy's been my guardian since I was four years old when our parents were killed in a plane crash. Our dad was a good pilot, but something went wrong with the plane, and it went down. Aunt Ellen came to live with us a couple of months later to help out while Amy worked."

"You were only four?" Tobey asked in surprise, thinking that Amy must have been very young for such a big responsibility.

Gretchen nodded. "That was ten years ago. Amy was twenty-one—she's a lot older than I am. How old are you?"

Amy shook her head in exasperation, but Tobey answered matter-of-factly, "I'm twenty-eight."

"Really? You don't look it."

He almost sighed himself. Glancing at Amy, he replied, "So I've been told."

"Tobey, do you like onions and peppers?" Ellen asked, poking her head in the door.

"Yes, ma'am," he answered with a smile.

"Mushrooms?"

"Love 'em."

She disappeared again, leaving Tobey to murmur, "I really wish she wouldn't go to this much trouble."

Amy shrugged as she swallowed a forkful of her own dinner. "She really doesn't mind."

"You're not married, are you, Tobey?" Gretchen asked, still visibly curious about him.

"No." That was a painful line of conversation he really didn't want to pursue, so he turned the questioning around rather quickly. "What grade are you in, Gretchen?"

"I'll be starting ninth grade in a couple of weeks. I want Amy to let me go to a race before school starts, but she's always afraid I'll get in her way, even though I've promised I wouldn't." Gretchen gave her sister an annoyed look.

"If it's okay with your sister, maybe I can make arrangements for you to attend a race soon," Tobey offered impulsively, hoping Amy wouldn't get mad. "There are plenty of kids your age among the driver and crew families. I'm sure we could find a safe place for you to watch the race without interfering with Amy's responsibilities."

The girl's face lit up. "Seriously? That would be so cool! Could I, Amy?"

Amy glanced at Tobey with an expression he couldn't quite interpret. "We'll talk about it."

Before Gretchen could press her case, Ellen returned with a plate overflowing with one of the biggest omelets Tobey had ever seen. Apparently, she'd been serious when she'd speculated that he was starving.

"Wow, this is…"

"Large, I know," Ellen finished for him with a slight laugh. "I have a hard time cooking just a little. Don't feel that you have to eat it all."

He took a generous bite as she seated herself across

the table with her own cooling meal. "I don't think you'll have to throw any of it away," he said after swallowing. "This is delicious. And since all I had for lunch was a bag of chips and a candy bar out of the vending machine, I guess I'm hungrier than I'd realized."

Ellen looked both pleased by the compliment and disapproving of his admission. "You sound like Amy. Too busy to stop and eat a decent meal. I keep telling her she works too hard—sounds like you're in the same habit."

"This week has been particularly demanding," he replied. "It's been a challenge, to say the least."

"And speaking of which, we need to work one more radio interview into your schedule for Friday afternoon," Amy said, looking at him from across the table. "I set it up this afternoon. From the itinerary you gave me, it looked as though you had a half hour free at about two-thirty."

Mentally reviewing his schedule, Tobey groaned softly. "That half hour was my only chance to sit down and breathe for a minute Friday afternoon."

"You'll have to wait and breathe on Monday," she said without apparent sympathy. "Payton Reese really wants to interview you before the race, and Friday afternoon seemed to be the only time available for both of you."

"Geez, Amy, give the guy a break," Gretchen stated. "You're not his boss, are you?"

Amy's eyes narrowed, and Tobey spoke quickly to spare the younger girl a certain scolding. "When it comes to PR stuff, Amy calls the shots. I'll note the interview on my calendar—and I won't be late," he added with a rueful glance at Amy. "I know how important this is."

She nodded, not quite succeeding in hiding her lingering annoyance with her sister. "I don't know if you've checked your e-mail this afternoon, but I forwarded you a memo from Gavin Webber at Vittle Farms. You'll want to read it before you talk to anyone in the media. He gave us several good quotes you can work in about Vittle Farms' faith in you and the team."

Eating steadily, Tobey continued to listen and nod while Amy outlined nearly every minute of the upcoming race weekend. "Making sure they were on the same page," as she put it. Occasionally Gretchen or Ellen would try to interject a non-business-related topic, only to be quelled by a look from Amy.

"I have strawberry shortcake for dessert," Ellen said when Tobey had eaten the last bite of the huge omelet. "Please don't tell me you're allergic to strawberries."

"I'm not," he assured her with a smile. "But I am pretty full."

She was already on her feet, motioning for everyone else to remain seated as she headed for the kitchen. "Oh, surely you can hold just a bite of dessert."

"She really does make good shortcake," Gretchen said.

Though he figured he'd regret it later, Tobey vowed to eat at least part of his dessert, just because it seemed to make Ellen so happy to feed him. "How do you keep from being blimps if she always pushes food like this?" he asked Amy in a low voice.

"She's able to restrain herself unless we have

company for dinner," Amy murmured in return. "Then it's full steam ahead and forget the calories."

"I like it when we have company," Gretchen confided ingenuously. "I'd much rather have strawberry short-cake for dessert than the healthy puddings and fruit and stuff Amy always insists on."

Tobey nodded sympathetically. "I've got a real taste for sugar and junk food myself. But I try to eat healthy—for the most part."

"Treats taste even better when they're an indulgence rather than a regular thing," Ellen added cheerfully, carrying in a tray of dessert dishes holding shortcake smothered in fresh strawberries and what looked to be hand-whipped cream topping.

With a mental vow to try to choose healthy foods at the track on the coming weekend—not an easy thing to do when surrounded by food, as the team always seemed to be—Tobey dug in.

"You have a very nice family," Tobey said when Amy walked him out to his car soon after dinner on the pretext of telling him one last thing about the weekend's public relations schedule.

His comment gave her the perfect opening for what she'd intended to say when she offered to walk him out. "Thank you. It occurred to me only after I saw your expression when you arrived that I hadn't mentioned we'd be dining with my great-aunt and my sister. I'm sorry, I thought you knew they lived with me."

"No. I don't actually know much about you at all," he

admitted, leaning against his car for a moment as he studied her face. It was still mostly light on that long summer day, so she had no trouble seeing the curiosity in his blue eyes. "You and I haven't spent a lot of time together during the past year, and when we did, we talked business. I had no idea you've been raising your little sister for so long. That must have been difficult for you."

"It was easier having Aunt Ellen to help," she replied with a slight shrug. She saw no need to get into just how hard it had been to find herself suddenly responsible for a four-year-old when she'd been only twenty-one. Overwhelmed with grief, terrified about the future, feeling completely unprepared, she had accepted with gratitude and relief when Aunt Ellen had offered to help out. Now their aunt was getting older and Amy was the one who shouldered much of the responsibility. And sometimes she still felt overwhelmed.

"I like your aunt. Your little sister, too."

She forced a smile. "You saw them on their best behavior tonight. But as it happens, I like them, too."

His gaze focused on her mouth, as if studying her smile. Suddenly self-conscious, she felt her smile start to fade and she glanced away.

No way was she going to complicate this situation even further by letting Tobey see her attraction to him, she vowed. It was bad enough that she would be fretting after he left about whether he had misinterpreted her impulsive invitation to dinner. Would he have arrived bearing wine if he had known all along that they would be joined by her aunt and sister?

"As you've pointed out, we'll be working closely together from now on," Tobey said, reaching for his door handle. "I'm sure we'll get to know each other pretty well."

"I suppose so," she agreed carefully. On a business basis, of course, she added silently.

There was nothing businesslike about the look he gave her as he climbed into his car. "I'm looking forward to it," he said and closed the door before she could answer.

Not that she knew exactly what she would have said, anyway, she thought, watching him drive away.

Gretchen was waiting just inside the door when Amy went back inside. "Oh, my gosh, Tobey is so-o-o cute," she enthused, her topaz eyes gleaming. "He looks like he should be on TV or something. His eyes are so blue. Do you think he wears contacts?"

"I have no idea," Amy replied, trying to sound as though she hadn't wondered the same thing herself once or twice. "It's not something we've ever discussed."

Gretchen planted her hands on her slender hips and gave her sister a stern look. "Don't even try to tell me you haven't noticed how cute Tobey is."

Amy hesitated a moment, then shrugged in resignation. "Of course I've noticed. I'm not blind. He's very attractive."

"*Thank* you," Gretchen exclaimed in satisfaction. "So? Are you going to do anything about it?"

"What do you mean?"

"He's single, right? And you're single. You seemed

to hit it off pretty well over dinner, even though you were kind of boring, talking about business all the time."

"I wasn't boring." Amy turned toward the den, hearing Gretchen following behind her. "I talked about business because it was a business dinner. I told you that before he even arrived."

"Well, yeah, that was a great way to get him here." Gretchen plopped onto the couch, already reaching for the TV remote. "But you don't have to talk business all the time, you know? Maybe you'd find out you have some more stuff in common if you'd just make a little effort."

Shaking her head, Amy sat in a chair and picked up the laptop computer she'd set beside it earlier. When she was in town and not out for business meetings or work events, she was in the habit of answering e-mail in the den for an hour or so after dinner while Gretchen watched television. Sometimes Aunt Ellen joined them, but usually she preferred to read in her room after dinner. Amy had always suspected Aunt Ellen was giving the sisters that time to spend together in their otherwise hectic days.

Amy had learned to treasure these hours. Though ostensibly both she and Gretchen were occupied with other things, this was the time when they talked. During commercial breaks, Gretchen would often bring up a topic of conversation, often idle gossip about school or her friends, but occasionally a more serious subject that she'd wanted to discuss with her sister. It seemed easier for her to broach those topics during these casual, after-dinner chats than at any other time.

"Are you seriously trying to fix me up with Tobey?" Amy asked, glancing up as her computer booted.

"Why not? He's too old for me. And he's too cute to let him go to waste," Gretchen quipped.

"I doubt that Tobey's going to waste," Amy replied dryly. "Besides, he's a little young for me."

Gretchen made a sound of exasperation. "Three years? That's nothing. I think he could be just what you need. You're not going to stay single forever, are you? End up like Aunt Ellen?"

Amy looked quickly at the doorway, hoping their great-aunt hadn't heard that thoughtless remark. "Gretchen! Aunt Ellen has had a wonderful life. She would be very hurt if she heard you using her as an example of what not to become."

"I didn't mean it like that," Gretchen insisted, though she, too, looked guiltily toward the doorway. "I just think it would be cool if you could find someone to fall in love with, you know? You're always looking after me and now that I'm almost an adult, I think it's time for you to have a little fun. Even Aunt Ellen thinks so. I heard her say so to her friend Betty on the phone the other day."

Amy winced. "Both you and Aunt Ellen know how hard I worked to get this promotion. As demanding as it is, this is a dream job for me, and I need to concentrate on it for the rest of the season, at least. I barely have time to sleep, much less to get involved with anyone right now, and I'm okay with that. Really. As for taking care of you, that's been a privilege, not a chore."

Gretchen's cheeks darkened, as they always did when Amy tried to get "mushy." "My show's on," she said, focusing her attention on the television screen, where a young man with flowing hair and soulful eyes appeared to be running for his life from a gang of bad guys.

Identifying the scene as from a popular teen-targeted adventure series, Amy turned her own attention back to the computer screen. She hoped devoutly that Gretchen would forget her matchmaking scheme as quickly as she had hatched it.

TOBEY WENT STRAIGHT back to the shop after dinner. He had at least another couple of hours to put in that evening. He'd be lucky to get in five or six hours' sleep before his trip to New York the next day. Not that he thought he'd be able to sleep much even if he found the time.

Nerves were beginning to eat at him, to his annoyance. He was ready for this job, he reminded himself. He'd been training for it almost his whole life. His dedication to it had kept him away from his family back home in Tennessee to the extent that he hardly knew his nieces and nephews. It had come between him and old friends. And it had been the reason his youthful engagement had ended in a painful, and ultimately tragic manner. Screwing up now would make all of those old sacrifices meaningless, he thought somberly.

Working with Neil had given him the experience and the knowledge to put to work as crew chief for the upcoming race. He'd pored over notes from past races, made copious notes of his own, studied and consulted and obsessed—there was nothing more he could do to prepare himself.

The car and backup car were already at the track, stowed safely in the back of the team hauler. Jesse Herrington, Kent's driver, had left that morning so Kent's motor home would be set up, stocked and ready when Kent arrived at the track tomorrow. Tobey would be staying at a hotel, since the motor home he'd ordered only a few days earlier wouldn't be delivered until Monday. There hadn't been time for him to order a new one, nor did he think he could justify that expense yet, but with Dawson's assistance, he'd acquired a very nice, three-year-old, forty-two-foot motor home that would serve him well for the remainder of the season.

Drivers and crew chiefs had found that having their own motor home at the track saved commuting time, as well as giving them a private, quiet place to crash whenever they had a blessed few minutes free. It was expensive, of course, not only in the cost of purchasing and maintaining the luxury RVs, but also employing someone to drive the behemoths to the various tracks and keep them stocked to the owners' tastes. Tobey had already hired a retired husband-and-wife team to drive his motor home beginning next week; once they'd set up at a track, they would stay in a hotel, leaving the motor home for Tobey's use until after the race.

It still stunned him that he could afford such a luxury. His salary had more than tripled with his promotion. He wasn't in this job for the money; the hours were too long, the stress too high, the work too demanding to do it for anything but the love of the sport. But it was nice to be well compensated for the effort, he thought with a wry smile. Now all he had to do was prove he was worth the investment.

"Hey, chief?"

He wondered if he'd ever get tired of hearing *that*. "Yeah, Joey, what is it?"

The newly promoted car chief—giving Joey Holman that job had been Tobey's first official act after taking over the team—strolled into the office with a small stack of papers that he tossed onto the desk with a flourish. Joey's naturally florid face glowed with satisfaction when he said, "There you go. I told you I'd have it finished before we left."

Tobey glanced at his watch. "Cutting it pretty close."

"Yeah, but I made it. So, you going to get any sleep tonight?"

"Some. You?"

"Just leaving now. I figure I can work in about six hours before catching the plane tomorrow. Have you had dinner?"

"Yeah. Amy and I went over the PR schedule during dinner."

"That Amy." Joey shook his shaggy red head. "I've got to admit, I don't know her very well, but I've never heard her talk about anything but business. It's like she lives and breathes the job, you know?"

"Don't we all?"

"Well, yeah, but at least we take breaks sometimes. You know, hang out in the parking lot to shoot hoops for a few minutes to unwind. Grab a beer and watch a game in the hauler office. Kent takes time to hang out with us and play video games every once in a while, when he's not slipping away for extra time with his fiancée. Even you've been known to goof off occasionally, and let's face it, you're a workaholic. But Amy, I've never seen her without her phone at her ear. Never heard her say anything that didn't have to do with work. Did she loosen up any during dinner?"

"We had a very nice dinner with her great-aunt and her kid sister," Tobey said with a shrug. "But, yeah, we mostly talked business. After all, we leave for New York first thing in the morning. There were several last-minute details to talk about."

Joey looked vaguely surprised. "How'd you end up at a family dinner?"

"She lives with them. Or they live with her, I'm not sure. Anyway, I guess it was more convenient for her to have me join them for the meal than to try to carve out time for another meeting this evening. And it was nice. Haven't had a home-cooked meal in a while, and her great-aunt is a fantastic cook."

He saw no need to mention the shellfish mix-up. Or the wine that no one drank. Actually, he didn't know why he was talking about this at all, except that Joey was probably his closest friend on the team. They'd bonded through a couple of difficult years with Neil, who'd been in the habit of firing both of them regularly, with Kent habitually stepping in to get them rehired. Joey might have been hired because he was Dawson Ritter's nephew, but he was one of the hardest-working and most competent members of the team.

Joey seemed to think Tobey's explanation of the dinner arrangements made sense. "So she talks business even during family meals. Not surprising. It's why she's so good at the job, I guess." He changed the subject. "I'm about to head out. Anything else you need before I go?"

"No, this will do it. Get some rest."

"You do the same. You're going to need it this weekend." Joey paused in the doorway to look searchingly back at his friend. "How are you feeling about the upcoming race, Tob? A little nervous?"

Tobey hesitated. His first instinct was to deny any nerves, repeat the confidently optimistic lines Amy had given him to say whenever anyone asked if he felt up to his new responsibilities. But this was Joey. And his friend deserved the truth. "Honestly? I'm tied in knots. You know what's going to happen if anything goes wrong this weekend? Everyone's going to say they never should have dumped Neil for me."

"That's hardly the way it happened," Joey countered loyally.

"Yeah, but that's what they'll say."

"Yeah," Joey agreed after a moment. "You're right. Lot of pressure on you, man."

Tobey drew a deep breath. "True. But this is what I've been working toward for my whole career. I'm ready as I'm ever going to be. How about you?"

"You won't regret making me car chief," Joey

promised as he moved into the hallway. "I've sacrificed too much to get here to blow it now."

Tobey nodded somberly, letting that serve as his only reply. He knew all too much about making sacrifices. And no matter how much he accomplished with this team, how many victories or championships would come in his career, there would always be a tiny, haunting voice inside him that wondered if it had truly been worth what he'd lost.

CHAPTER FOUR

KENT HAD INVITED Tobey and Amy to fly on his private plane Thursday morning, giving them a chance to discuss schedules and strategies one last time before the hectic weekend began. Sometimes Kent's fiancée, Tanya Wells, accompanied them, but her own schedule had been full that weekend. A popular wedding photographer, Tanya was kept busy juggling the responsibilities of her career with the never-ending demands of Kent's.

It wasn't easy being involved with the reigning champion of NASCAR. Between the extensive traveling, the exhausting publicity agenda, the practicing and testing, team meetings and relentless scrutiny of the fans and media, there was little time left for a personal life. Tobey had watched Kent and Tanya on occasion, wondering how they managed to hold their relationship together despite everything. He'd wondered the same about the other long-term relationships in the sport.

What kept some of them together through all the ups and downs they encountered through the years while so many other unions disintegrated under the stress? How were some people able to focus on the job and on their personal relationships when so many, himself included, failed miserably?

Even Kent's parents, NASCAR Sprint Cup Series driver Dean Grosso and his wife and business partner, Patsy, were having problems in their marriage. Gossip had it that, after more than thirty years of combining marriage, family and racing, there was quite a bit of tension between Dean and Patsy this season. He had heard a rumor that Patsy had moved out. It was a sad situation, and Tobey knew it preyed on Kent's mind. Part of Tobey's job was to try to keep the driver focused on winning despite the problems he faced in his private life.

Even during the flight, Amy could hardly finish a sentence to Kent or Tobey before her phone notified her of a call or text message or e-mail, sometimes all at once, it seemed. Tobey listened in as she confirmed appointments, scheduled others for upcoming weeks, turned down requests for interviews and appearances she couldn't fit into the calendar or that she didn't deem advantageous. Occasionally she consulted Kent about whether he was interested in one opportunity or another, but generally he left that sort of decision to her. Amy was well compensated to put Kent's best public foot forward and as far as Tobey could tell, Kent trusted her implicitly.

He wished he could be confident that Kent felt the same way about him. Sure, Kent said all the right things about Tobey's qualifications as crew chief. And it had been as much Kent's decision as Dawson's to promote Tobey when they had to let Neil go. But Tobey was well aware that there had been an element of desperation in that promotion.

This late in the season, there had been no time for interviewing, screening or acclimating a new crew chief. He had been available, familiar with the team and its practices and ready to step in. It was up to him now to prove they hadn't made a mistake by giving him this chance.

"Tobey? Did you hear me?"

Both Amy and Kent were looking at him quizzically when her question caught his attention. He roused himself with an effort. "Sorry, Amy. I got distracted for a minute. What did you say again?"

"I said *NASCAR Nites* wants to interview you and Kent in California. Just a short fluff piece about the men behind the public masks. What you're like when you aren't working. Your hobbies, interests, love lives— that sort of thing the fans like."

Tobey wasn't quite able to repress a laugh. "It's going to be a real short interview on my part. Crew chiefs don't have time for hobbies, interests *or* a love life. The writers need to just talk to the drivers about that sort of thing."

Kent snorted good-humoredly. "Yeah, right. Try telling Tanya about all my spare time for our love life and she'll pull a muscle laughing hysterically."

"It's a shame she couldn't join you this weekend," Amy said. "Upstate New York is such a beautiful, romantic area with all the lakes and streams and waterfalls so close to the track."

Kent cocked an eyebrow. "So you've had a few romantic encounters there, have you?"

"Me?" She did a credible imitation of his snort. "Hardly. The closest relationship I've had at a race track was with my cell phone."

"You really should bring your family to a race soon," Tobey reminded her. "They would probably enjoy watching you work."

"Your aunt and your sister?" Kent apparently knew more about Amy's personal life than Tobey had until only the night before. "You *should* bring them, Amy. I'd like to meet them."

So Tobey was one up on Kent in that respect, he mused, then frowned, wondering why that irrelevant thought had even occurred to him.

"I'll try to bring them before the season's over," Amy said. "I've been concerned that they would interfere with my work, or that they'd feel neglected because I couldn't pay much attention to them, but they would probably be fine."

"Sure they will," Tobey agreed. "Will Branch's PR rep, Kylie Palmer, brings her son to the tracks all the time. Lots of other people have their families at the tracks and still manage to do their jobs."

"Oh, yeah," Kent muttered, his smile suddenly fading. "The family that races together stays together, isn't that what they say?"

Knowing that Kent was thinking about his parents, Tobey quickly brought up a question about their strategy for this road race track that was so different from the usual racing venues. He knew the answer before Kent even replied, but it was a way to get the driver's mind off his personal issues and back on the job. And that was advice he needed to take for himself, he thought, dragging his gaze firmly away from Amy's pretty face.

FROM THE MOMENT they arrived at the race track, Amy, Kent and Tobey were on the run, inundated by their respective responsibilities. Amy, as usual, was rarely far from Kent's side when he wasn't in his race car.

She was with him at interviews, appearances and autograph sessions, standing just behind him with her Internet-connected cell phone in hand, keeping him on task and on schedule. She whispered advice in his ear, reminded him of names he had forgotten, told him which way to look and to smile when he became distracted, and firmly redirected lines of questioning that became uncomfortable or too personal. Amy gladly played the "bad cop," willing to be seen as difficult herself rather than let her driver be viewed in a less than positive light.

Sometimes Tobey joined them when the event called for both driver and crew chief to appear. Despite his own hectic schedule, he was scrupulously punctual for the appointments. He learned his lessons quickly, she thought in secret amusement.

She was still trying to decide exactly how she felt about Tobey, aside from his undeniable physical attractiveness. Maybe it would be easier to reach a conclusion if she didn't have the nagging feeling that there was too much about him she still didn't know.

She saw the calm, competent, pleasant face he wore

to work every day. She could tell how much his job meant to him, and how hard he was willing to work to be successful in it. She felt as though she were watching him evolve when it came to being more expressive and articulate with the media, another aspect of his new, heightened responsibilities. Yet she knew little about him personally other than the official biography they had worked up together when he'd received his promotion.

Tobias Ray Harris, twenty-eight, had grown up in eastern Tennessee, the third child and only son of a rural pastor, now deceased, and a schoolteacher mother, now remarried and living in Nashville. He said he'd once dreamed of being a driver, but had decided he was more suited to the pits than the cockpit—he'd seemed quite proud of that quip. He had started out like so many hopeful youngsters, sweeping floors in the garage, and with single-minded determination had risen through the ranks, eventually putting himself into the position where he was the logical choice to fill in for the former crew chief.

Those things she knew, along with the fact that he was single and not currently involved with anyone—or so he'd told the last gossip columnist who'd asked. What she didn't know was who he was when he wasn't on the job, though he seemed to always be at work. She knew that because she was, too, she thought wryly.

Tobey seemed like a hardworking, ambitious, pleasant-natured, affable guy, but she suspected there was more to him than he allowed most people to see. A wall of reserve he'd built around a part of himself that he kept very private.

Or was she only romanticizing him because she was so inexplicably fascinated by him? Maybe he was exactly what he seemed to be, with nothing beneath the surface except a man who loved his job almost to the exclusion of all else.

"How did I do?"

Brought out of her thoughts of him by the sound of his voice behind her, Amy turned with a slight start. "You did fine," she assured him, referring to the interview he had just completed. "You handled every question just right."

He made a show of wiping his brow. "I can't say I'll ever really like this part of the job, but I think I'll get better at it with practice."

"Of course you will," she assured him.

They stood outside the hauler where the interview had taken place. Activity bustled all around them, though the noise hardly registered to Amy, since the decibel level was significantly lower than when the cars were screaming around the track. She had grown accustomed to the chaos that was a part of being at the track during a race weekend. She hardly even noticed when someone bumped her on the way into the hauler, merely stepping aside and nodding absently in response to a muttered apology.

Tobey reached out to steady her, his hand lingering a moment on her arm before he let it fall. Just long enough to make her pulse rate jump a little in response to his touch, something that made her frown before she quickly smoothed the expression back into a bland smile. "Well, anyway…"

"Do you have plans for dinner?"

Caught off guard by the question, she shook her head. "I was going to have dinner in my room while I go over some notes for tomorrow."

"That sounds boring. Why don't you join us instead?"

"Us?"

He nodded. "Kent, Dawson, Anna and me. We're dining over at the harbor. I've never eaten at this restaurant, but Kent told me it's really good. I'm sure he and Dawson would both like for you to come with us, and I know Anna would appreciate having another woman there."

She had no doubt that she would be welcome. She had dined with Kent and the team owner and his delightful wife on several occasions before. Yet it still surprised her that Tobey seemed so eager for her to join them tonight. She couldn't help wondering if it was because he was a bit nervous about dining with the driver and owner on the eve of qualifying for this first race with him as crew chief.

She knew it had been routine for Neil to eat with Kent and Dawson the first night at a venue. They would all be aware of his absence tonight. Perhaps Tobey thought her presence would put everyone more at ease.

"Okay," she said with a nod. After all, this was one of her responsibilities, she told herself. Keeping the team happy and comfortable together, especially out in public. "Sounds good. When are you going?"

He glanced at his watch. "I'm supposed to meet them in half an hour. I've got a rental car. Why don't you ride with me and I'll take you back to the hotel afterward."

They, along with several other team members, were staying at the same hotel, reservations having been made from headquarters. Nearby rooms were always at a premium during race weekends, so the various teams booked blocks of rooms sometimes more than a year in advance of the events.

Amy knew Dawson had helped Tobey acquire a motor home for the remainder of the season, so this would be his last weekend in a hotel room. Life had definitely changed overnight for the former crew chief's assistant. She hoped the promotion wouldn't go to his head. She rather liked the unassuming, modest man she'd always thought him to be.

"Just let me get a couple of things out of the hauler and I'll be ready to go."

He nodded, his expression as pleasantly unreadable as ever. "Take your time."

"A SEAFOOD PLACE?" Amy asked Tobey as they walked into the nautically themed restaurant on the banks of Seneca Lake. "Isn't that sort of risky for you, considering your shellfish allergy?"

He shrugged, looking a bit uncomfortable at the reminder of the menu faux pas at her house. "I'll order carefully. I just have to mention to the server that I need to avoid any risk of cross-contamination."

Okay, so his food allergy was another topic he was sensitive about. With some relief, she spotted Kent and the Ritters sitting at a table across the room. "Looks like the others are already here."

"Yeah, I see them." Nodding toward their party when the hostess approached them, Tobey stood back to allow Amy to precede him to the table.

Dawson and Kent both stood when Amy joined them, Dawson out of deeply ingrained old-fashioned manners, Kent probably following the lead of his boss, since he wasn't usually so formal around her. Anna Ritter held out a thin, blue-veined hand covered in glittering rings. "Amy. We're so glad you could join us tonight."

Figuring that Tobey had let the others know she was coming, Amy clasped the older woman's hand with a warm smile. "It's good to see you, Anna. Are you feeling better?"

Anna brushed off the question with a slight laugh. "Much, thank you. Dawson exaggerated how badly I was ill last week. It was just a lousy cold."

"I'm glad it was nothing serious." Amy gave Tobey a smile of gratitude when he held a chair for her before taking his own next to her.

Sixtyish Anna Ritter was addicted to glitter of all kinds. Her dyed-gold hair, her rhinestone-decorated plastic glasses, her earrings, necklace, bracelets, watch, rings, sequin-splashed clothes…everything about her sparkled and twinkled, including her merry brown eyes.

In contrast to his flashy wife, Dawson Ritter was almost nondescript. With his balding head, prominent ears and thick bifocal glasses, he didn't look like the powerful, multimillionaire trucking mogul that he was. Yet after that first innocuous impression, most people figured out pretty quickly that Dawson was a man to be reckoned with, fully in control of his business holdings and the racing team he had owned for several years.

He was a very nice man, and generally easygoing, but push him too far and he pushed back hard. That was what Neil had eventually discovered when he'd shown up for work one too many times hungover and bad-tempered.

Amy liked both the Ritters, though she couldn't claim to know either of them well. Still, in the past year, she had seen enough of them to understand that they were a friendly, generous and genuine couple who were devoted to each other and very loyal to the hundreds of people who depended on them.

Dawson announced that dinner was on him and insisted everyone should order lavishly. "You're all going to need the sustenance this weekend," he said, only mostly joking. "We're going to be running nonstop starting at dawn."

"Starting?" Kent shook his head. "I've been running since I stepped off the plane this morning, thanks to Amy's insane PR schedule."

"You have to admit I got you some good exposure," she shot back. "That interview with the national morning show was a real coup."

He nodded. "I could have done without the rehash of the college fiasco, but yeah."

It bothered her that the reminder brought a grim look to his eyes for a moment. Amy took her responsibilities to Kent very seriously. Maybe too much so at times, she thought as she looked over the menu. Oddly enough, she'd begun to feel a bit maternal about her charge, even though he was only a few months her junior. It was her job to smooth his way professionally. Keep the client happy. Was it any wonder she sometimes fretted about his personal problems, as well?

He'd had a tough season, that was for certain. Though he had somehow managed to race well enough to place himself among the top ten points positions, he had done so despite the off-the-track obstacles he'd encountered since February.

The season had started with a problem of some sort between Kent and Tanya. Amy had never heard the details, but she'd known even then that something was wrong and she'd worried that the couple known as "NASCAR's sweethearts" had been close to splitting up. Fortunately that had been resolved, and Kent and Tanya had announced their engagement, both glowing with happiness.

During that same time, Kent had admitted in an interview that he'd been asked to leave State University during his freshman year there for cheating on a major test. It wasn't something he was proud of, he'd said, having been so ashamed of his actions that he'd covered it up for years. But he *was* proud that he had turned his life around, earning a degree from a reputable technical college and staying scrupulously ethical in both his professional and personal conduct since that one misjudgment.

Kent had warned Amy ahead of time—though by less than twelve hours—what he'd planned to say in that revealing interview, giving her a heads-up on the spin she would have to put on his confession. He had not, however, told her what had made him decide to make his record public at that particular time, except to say that it was bound to come out sometime and he wanted to control where, when and how.

She had wondered ever since if there had been more to the story. Had the tabloids got hold of the story? Maybe someone threatened Kent with that information in some way? If there had been an effort to blackmail him or in some other way use the story to embarrass him, he had never let on.

Thanks to Kent's candor and Amy's careful handling of the confession, the minor gossip tempest that had followed had been short-lived. It had fired up again, however, when Neil Sanchez was summarily released in midseason, always a reason for tongues to wag in this sport. Combined with the not-so-secret tensions between Kent's highly visible parents and the scandal of his sister, Sophia, getting involved with Justin Murphy, both a fierce competitor and a family enemy, Kent had plenty to worry about in addition to his driving.

"Your sponsors approve of the way you've handled everything this season," Amy assured him warmly.

"As do I," Dawson confirmed with a nod. "Don't let yourself get distracted with outside stuff now, boy. Just concentrate on qualifying tomorrow and racing Sunday and everything else will take care of itself."

Having given them plenty of time to exchange greetings and look over the menu, the nautically dressed server approached to ask if they were ready to order appetizers. Taking advantage of the restaurant's specialties, everyone but Tobey ordered seafood. Both the Ritters requested shrimp cocktails, while Amy asked for shrimp gumbo and Kent ordered steamed clams. Tobey opted for buffalo wings.

"I'm thinking about having the New York strip steak topped with scampi au jus butter for an entrée," Dawson said, peering at the menu through his thick lenses.

Anna clucked disapprovingly and shook her head, causing her dangling earrings to sparkle like tiny chandeliers. "Think of your cholesterol," she reminded him. "How about this nice salmon dish instead?"

Dawson frowned at her. "I eat healthy all week. Tonight I'm splurging. I'll make up for it on the stationary bike tomorrow."

"Sounds like a plan to me," Kent seconded eagerly. "I'll have the steak and lobster tail. Heavy on the drawn butter."

Anna sighed again, muttering something about men beneath her breath before declaring that she would have the seafood pasta. Amy and Tobey shared an amused look. Anna's choice was drenched in a creamy Alfredo sauce which, while probably delicious, could hardly be considered a light dish.

"Well, Tobey?" Amy asked. "Are you going to be bad tonight, too?"

Holding her gaze with his own, he gave her a faint, slightly crooked smile. "It's certainly tempting," he murmured.

She swallowed hard, telling herself he was only talking about food. He couldn't have meant the double entendre his sexy drawl implied, at least to her ears.

She looked quickly at her menu, hoping the sudden warmth in her cheeks wasn't visible to the others. "The rainbow trout sounds good," she said, glancing over the description of lemon-and-butter seared trout served with sautéed apples and almonds over steamed rice. If everyone else was going to pretend butter was a health food tonight, she figured she might as well go along.

Tobey selected the barbecued ribs served with a house-specialty sauce. Amy heard him say something in a low tone to the server, and while she couldn't hear the words, she figured he was relaying his warning about cross-contamination. It must be annoying to have to deal with a dangerous food allergy, she mused, glad she hadn't had to worry about that for herself or her little sister. The only allergies they'd had to contend with other than Gretchen's sensitivity to ginger were ragweed and pollen, and those were irritating enough during the peak of hay fever season.

She suspected that she was the only other person at the table who knew about Tobey's allergy. Something about that seemed oddly intimate. Almost as if he knew what she was thinking, Tobey gave her a slight smile when the server moved away.

Feeling her cheeks go warm again, she looked quickly away, trying to keep her thoughts strictly focused on business for the duration of the meal.

THE MAXIMUS MOTORSPORTS team rooms had been reserved in a block, so Amy and Tobey were on the same floor of the hotel. They saw other members of the team milling downstairs when they returned from dinner, and they stopped a couple of times to talk with them before getting onto the elevator.

Tobey's room was farther down the hallway from the elevator than Amy's. He'd told her he wanted to be at the track at five the next morning, so he was planning to turn in early tonight. She planned to sleep in a bit later, though admittedly not much later.

Key card in hand, she paused in front of her door. "Thanks for inviting me to dinner, Tobey," she said, trying to keep both her tone and her expression casual. "I really enjoyed it."

"So did I. We'll have to do it again sometime."

"I'm sure we'll be eating a lot of meals together now that you're crew chief," she replied with a slight shrug. "I joined Kent and Neil often to discuss schedules and strategies."

"Oh, yeah. That, too."

Puzzled, she asked, "What did you mean?"

"I thought maybe you and I could have dinner sometime. You know. Just the two of us."

Her voice seemed to jam in her throat as she tried to come up with a response to that. Tried to figure out exactly what he meant by proposing a dinner for two. "Sure, we could do that sometime," she managed to say finally, keeping her tone as vague as his suggestion.

After all, she figured, if he was just talking about a one-on-one business discussion, that would be fine. That was her job, though she usually spent more time with the driver than the crew chief.

And if there had been a more personal angle to the invitation…well, she wouldn't be entirely opposed to that, either, though the idea made her nervous. Getting involved with a co-worker was never a good idea, especially now. She was still new enough in this job that she couldn't help worrying about doing something stupid and losing it. As the primary breadwinner for her family, she couldn't afford to do that. An involvement with the new crew chief sounded extremely risky—but she couldn't deny a certain chemistry between them. An unacknowledged awareness that had been there from the day they'd first met.

The smile he gave her had her wondering if maybe it might just be worth the risk to explore those feelings.

CHAPTER FIVE

IDEALLY, OF COURSE, Tobey would not have chosen to start his career as a crew chief in midseason, with the points race already well under way and everything riding on his first few races. And even under those circumstances, he certainly wouldn't have wished his first test to be a road race. As successful as Kent had been during the past few seasons, he had an abysmal record at the road races. He had a couple of DNFs and had never finished in the top five at the road tracks.

It didn't help either Tobey's confidence or Kent's that qualifying didn't go particularly well. Kent would be starting in the fourteenth position, and he'd barely been able to hold on to that spot. Seeing the grim look in his driver's eyes afterward, Tobey assured him heartily that everything would be fine.

"You drove the hell out of that track," he enthused. "We let you down with the car. It was too loose in the esses. We'll have that fixed by practice tomorrow, promise."

"I was too slow getting on the gas in Turn Four," Kent fretted.

"No way. You were great. You'll see when we get the car the way you like it."

What might have been the faintest glimmer of hope appeared in Kent's eyes. "You think?"

Tobey clapped him on the arm. "I know. You're the reigning NASCAR Sprint Cup Series champion, Grosso. You can tame this track."

"So, y'all work on that car."

Tobey nodded. "They're already on it. I'll go check."

"All right. I've got a thing…an interview. I've got to go change."

"Yeah. Call me when you're done."

Looking only slightly less discouraged, Kent headed for his motor home.

"You handled that very well."

Tobey turned in response to Amy's amused voice. She stood behind him, her always-present digital assistant in hand, a bulging tote bag hanging over her shoulder. She glanced in the direction in which Kent had disappeared into the milling crowds, then back at Tobey. "He looked like he needed that boost," she said.

"Yeah," he said with a slight shrug. "Everybody needs a pep talk every once in a while."

Her gaze narrowed on his face. "How about you? You starting to need a pep talk?"

"Me?" He gave her a broad grin. "Heck, no."

"Okay, then. I'll just say that I have no doubt that you're going to do a great job this weekend."

Because he didn't want her to see how much that vote of confidence meant to him, he simply said, "Thanks, Amy."

Her phone rang in her hand before she had a chance to say anything else. With a nod to him, she moved away, already deep into a discussion with whomever had called her.

TOBEY NEEDED a haircut, Amy thought incongruously, glancing back at him as he watched her walk away. His mop of blond-and-brown hair tumbled almost into his bright blue eyes, making him look ridiculously young and sexy. As the team's PR rep, it would not be out of line for her to remind him of the public image he wanted to project. The thing was, he looked so darned good, she wasn't going to say a word.

She wasn't the only one who'd noticed, of course. Tobey's new fame had gotten him plenty of attention from women race fans. There were already plenty who tried to catch Kent's attention, despite the public knowledge that he was engaged to be married. Tobey's admission that he was single had certainly brought out the hopeful admirers, she thought, glancing around at the lucky fans with passes that allowed them to be in the area during qualifying. Three young women nearby were pointing openly at Tobey, giggling and blushing as they posed to get his attention. To their disappointment, their efforts were futile. His mind was totally on his job today, just as it usually was, from Amy's observations.

She didn't believe for a moment that he wasn't as nervous about the upcoming race as Kent. But if his way of handling that stress was to pretend he didn't feel it, why should she argue with him?

He lifted a hand to wave to her, and she realized that he was well aware she was looking back at him as she walked away. And that she knew he was watching her in return. Swallowing hard, she dragged her gaze away and tried to pay attention again to the business call. "I'm sorry, what did you say?"

She really should be concerned that the new crew chief was affecting her formerly single-minded concentration. But she had to admit that she was rather enjoying the little ripples of awareness that went through her every time he smiled at her. It had been so long since she'd felt that way. So long since she had allowed herself to think about anything but her job and her responsibilities to her family. Maybe it was time for her to cut loose a little.

And maybe she was being a fool for even considering something like that when it came to Tobey Harris, she added with a frown, disconnecting the call with the woman from team headquarters. Because a flirtation gone wrong between them could cause more than problems in her job; she suspected he was just the kind of man who could leave a broken heart behind. Even a heart as well-guarded as her own.

EVERYTHING WAS so hectic during the remainder of Friday and all of Saturday that Amy and Tobey had no time alone together. They were always surrounded by team members, media, sponsor reps or fans. She stayed close to Kent when he wasn't in the car, making sure he had everything he needed, keeping him on schedule. She was busy enough that she was able to keep her reactions to Tobey under control for the most part, though she couldn't ignore an occasional jolt when their eyes met and he shot her a quick smile.

Practice went fairly well, but Kent's lap times still weren't as fast as he would have liked. From what Amy heard, he was somewhat more pleased with the car, though he still had some complaints about the handling in the turns known as "the esses." Tobey promised once again that the team would make sure the car was everything Kent wanted it to be during the race itself.

"Just keep telling me what you need," Amy heard him say after practice. "I'll make sure you get it."

Tobey certainly had the crew-chief pep talk down pat, she thought wryly. He sounded so confident that it was no wonder Kent looked a little more relaxed every time he talked to Tobey. Now if only the race went well Sunday. She saw the pressure reflected in the eyes of so many of the team members around her that weekend. How on earth could Tobey look so calm when so much was riding on this, his first big test?

She found out just how deceptive that calm demeanor was when she came upon him unexpectedly Sunday morning while everyone else was busy with various prerace preparations. She hadn't realized anyone was in the hauler lounge when she'd walked in to make a call. She knew Kent was at a public appearance and the rest of the team was in the garage or taking care of other business. Though the race was still a couple of hours away from starting, the infield was already loud and busy, driving her inside the hauler in search of relative quiet.

Tobey, whom she'd thought was with Kent, sat on the leather couch when she walked in, his face buried in his hands. She hadn't been trying for stealth, but apparently he hadn't heard her come in. He didn't move when she walked through the open door.

Uncertainly, she cleared her throat. He jumped almost completely off the couch in response.

"I'm sorry," she said quickly. "I didn't mean to startle you."

On his feet now, he pushed a hand through his shaggy hair and gave her a smile that was as attractive as it was fake. "No problem. Just grabbing a couple minutes away from the crazy out there. Is there something I can do for you?"

"No. I didn't realize you were in here. I was just going to make a call."

"Then I'll get out of your way."

Still wearing that bland smile, he started to move past her. She reached out impulsively to catch his arm. "Tobey?"

"Yeah?"

"Are you okay?"

His eyes widened just a little, the only sign that her question had caught him off guard. "I'm fine. Like I said, just catching a couple minutes of quiet before the race."

She searched his face, seeing telltale lines around his mouth that hinted at the stress he was under. Maybe it was time someone gave the crew chief a pep talk. "You're going to do a great job out there today, Tobey.

Dawson wouldn't have promoted you if he didn't think you could handle it."

"Dawson promoted me because there wasn't really time to find anyone else," he corrected her sardonically.

"That's not true. If he hadn't had faith in you, he wouldn't have risked the rest of the season. He had other options. He made the decision he thought was best."

He smiled down at her. "You seem to believe I'm in need of reassurance."

"I would be, if I were in your shoes," she admitted frankly.

He shook his head. "I'm fine, really. Totally ready for this."

"Yes, you're getting very good at saying that. I've taught you well, grasshopper."

His mouth twitched in response to the old TV reference. "Very funny."

"I'm glad you're so calm about today. It helps the rest of the team for you to be so confident."

"That's the game plan," he replied, and then gave a laugh that wasn't entirely steady. "I hope I'm convincing everyone else better than I'm fooling you. You're one of only two people who know I'm pretty much a wreck today."

She nodded to acknowledge his implicit admission that he wasn't as calm as he claimed to be. "You're doing a great job. Most people would never realize that you've got a case of performance panic."

He laughed again, a little more naturally this time. "I guess you're just better at reading people."

"Maybe I'm just better at reading *you,*" she teased in return.

Though she'd spoken the words lightly, for some reason they'd come out a little differently than she had intended. Tobey's gaze held hers as he murmured, "Yeah. Maybe you are."

She swallowed. "Um—"

Her phone rang in her hand. At almost the same time, Tobey's walkie-talkie squawked. "Hey, Tob," someone said. "Where you at, man? We need you in the garage."

"I'm on my way," he said.

Amy lifted her phone to her ear. "Amy Barber," she said, having been too flustered to look at the caller ID.

Tobey motioned toward the door, mouthing to her, "I'll see you later."

She nodded. "Break a leg," she whispered back, only half-aware of the woman verifying an interview in her ear.

He started to move toward the door, paused, then leaned over to brush a light kiss against her cheek. "For luck," he whispered, and then left the lounge before she could react.

"Amy?" her caller asked, sounding perplexed. "Are you still there? Have we been cut off?"

"No, uh, I'm still here, Kay," Amy managed to squeak out with some semblance of coherence. "What were you saying?"

She completed the call with her free hand pressed to the cheek Tobey had kissed.

TOBEY HAD DEBATED a long time about whether to continue a prerace tradition started by his predecessor. On the one hand, the team had come to expect it, and they were a superstitious bunch. On the other hand, it was the first race the team would run without Neil in charge, and Tobey kind of hated to remind them of that.

In the end, he and Kent had decided together that some traditions deserved to be preserved, just as Neil's many contributions to the team should be remembered and respected even now that he'd moved on. And so, Tobey, Kent, Steve and the rest of the track crew gathered in the pit stall just prior to the race as they always did. Dressed in their matching blue-and-red uniforms emblazoned with the Vittle Farms "Flying V" logo on their chests and names of secondary sponsors embroidered on patches down their sleeves, they held their safety helmets under their left arms as they extended their right arms and stacked their hands in the center of the huddle.

The chalky taste of an antacid still lingering in his mouth, Tobey drew a deep breath, feeling all those nervous but determined gazes focused on his face. He could do this, he reminded himself. His owner had faith in him, his driver and team had all pledged their support to his decisions…and Amy had said she had full confidence in him. He could still feel the softness of her cheek against his lips, could still recall the faintly floral scent of her hair as it had brushed against his face when he'd pulled away.

Letting that memory brace him, he raised his voice to be heard over the chaos surrounding him and his team. "Who are we?"

"Team 427," the teammates recited loudly.

"What do we do?"

"We race."

Shouting now, Tobey demanded, "Why are we here?"

Breaking into grins, they replied in eager yells, "To win!"

Cheering, they pumped their stacked hands once, then broke apart, dashing into positions for the start of the race. For the next several hours, they would perform as an efficient machine, all focused on one goal, all guided by Tobey's instructions.

Standing beside the car, Kent gave Tobey one quick, bracing nod before he donned his helmet. TV and print photographers jostled around them. Voices echoed over loudspeakers, and the excited fans in the stands were already cheering their favorites even before the engines were started. Outside the infield, vendors in open semi-trailers hawked souvenirs and memorabilia, while concessions sellers were doing a lively business.

The whole place was a blur of color and sound and activity and it took a great deal of concentration for the teams to focus on their jobs. But for the people who worked on those teams, one objective easily trumped those other distractions—getting their drivers to the front of the field when that checkered flag waved.

Tobey turned toward the pit box, excitement now replacing the nerves in his stomach. The pit box would serve as the command center during the race. He was joined beneath the sun-blocking awning by Joey and Ed, the chief engineer.

Communication was crucial during every race. Four laptop computers sat in front of them, while overhead monitors displayed weather information, car telemetry and positions and television race coverage. They donned sound-blocking headsets to allow them to communicate with each other, though Tobey and Steve, Kent's spotter, were the only ones who would talk directly with Kent in his car. Aware that the radio chatter was closely monitored by fans and media, they would be careful what they said, for the most part. For any instructions or changes Tobey wanted to keep confidential, he would use instant messaging, or have someone directly relay the information to the pit crew.

A polished, track-side TV reporter, followed by a pudgy, grubbier cameraman, paused beside the pit box to shout a question to Tobey. He pulled his headphones down around his neck long enough to give his packaged responses about how good the car was and how much faith he had in his driver and their team. At the last minute, he remembered to give the little wave he'd promised the high school tour group, something he'd seen Kent do earlier.

And then it was time for the race to start, and Tobey had eyes and ears for nothing but the No. 427 car.

AMY DIDN'T usually monitor the radio chatter through headphones during the races. She habitually watched the races on the TV screen in the hauler lounge while working on the computer and doing business on the phone. Because Kent was kept busy on race days right up until the green flag flew, she made use of the hours during the races to have some "alone time" to catch up on e-mails and phone messages.

She had a standing invitation to join the Ritters in the luxurious owner's suites and could climb to the top of the hauler whenever she wanted for a panoramic view of the track activities, but the lounge had become her preferred hideaway. Other team members were in and out of the lounge all during the events, but for the most part, she was the only one who camped there through the entire races. She could work in relative peace there, making and taking calls and e-mails while keeping up with the race on TV. Today, however, she found it hard to sit still, hard to concentrate on her own work when she knew how much was riding on the outcome of this race for both Kent and Tobey.

She winced as Kent narrowly avoided a couple of big wrecks, and grimaced after a bad pit stop that she knew would displease both Kent and Tobey. Still, they were doing pretty well, she noted optimistically. After miraculously recovering from that bad stop, Kent was managing to stay in the top fifteen positions, though he hadn't yet been able to lead a lap.

With a third of the race still to go, she drifted restlessly outside into the deafening roar of the cars and the crowd, her senses assaulted by the heat of the afternoon, the smells of fumes, beer and the barbecue grills scattered through the in-field campgrounds, the crush of people dashing from one place to another around her. She moved toward the pits, then paused where she could see Tobey on top of the pit box.

She noted that he was still holding on to his air of quiet confidence. She saw no visible tension in the set of his shoulders, no anxiety in his expression as he concentrated fiercely on the screens in front of him, the track ahead, the pit below and the voices talking through his headset.

"Hey, Amy."

She glanced around with a smile in response to the greeting from Josh Peeples, a young, part-time team member who'd been making himself indispensable to Tobey in hopes of being promoted to a full-time assistant position. Though he hoped to make pit crew soon, for now Josh served as "go-fer" for the team, dashing around the track with messages, fetching anything that was requested of him, sweeping, cleaning, anything that kept him visible and useful.

"Hi, Josh," she half yelled to make herself heard over the surrounding noise. "You think you could find me a headset?"

He nodded eagerly. "Hang on a sec. I'll see what I can do."

"I'd appreciate it."

A few minutes later, he was back, a headset in his hand, a smug smile on his face. "Here you go. You going to watch the rest from here?"

"No, I think I'll go to the top of the hauler. Thanks,

Josh." She turned and retraced her steps to the hauler, toward the ladder that would take her up to the vantage point above the crowds.

A railing around the top of the two-level hauler provided a safe barrier for the bird's-eye view. A couple of team members—an engineer and an engine specialist—huddled at the front, binoculars hanging from straps around their necks along with the official infield passes that everyone else, including Amy, had to wear at all times.

Someone had set up a couple of folding chairs beneath a canvas umbrella, but no one was making use of them. After nodding to the men, who didn't seem particularly surprised by her presence, even though she rarely joined them up there, she made herself comfortable. She wouldn't be able to hear her phone ring through the bulky headset, so she set it to vibrate and clipped it to the brown leather belt she wore with khaki slacks and a team polo shirt.

From her vantage point, she had a good view of the pits. Even from this high, she couldn't see the entire road track, but she could keep up with what was going on by listening to the chatter through her headset. She found herself paying the most attention to the things Tobey said, though Kent and Steve talked quite a bit, as well.

Kent had worked his way up to the sixth position. Leaving Rafael O'Bryan in the dust behind him, he moved into fifth as the crowd roared. The stress was beginning to show in Kent's voice when he screamed into the radio, "I'm loose! I'm loose in the turns."

"You're fine, Kent," Tobey replied, keeping his own tone calm and soothing. "Just hang in there and keep doing what you're doing."

"Where are we?"

"Twenty more laps, buddy. Plenty of time to get up front."

Steve shouted a warning as a cloud of smoke signaled trouble on the track ahead. "Low, Kent! Go low!"

"I'm *going* low! Damn it, I'm too loose."

"You can do this, Kent. You've got control. Just stay calm."

Tobey still sounded composed, but Amy thought she detected just the slightest hint of tension in his tone now.

"Caution's out. Caution's out," Steve chanted.

"Okay, Kent, bring 'er in to the pit. Four tires, guys. No mistakes. This race is going to end in a shoot-out."

"Four tires?" Amy heard the doubt in Kent's voice. "No way, Tobey, there's not time."

"Trust me, buddy, I'm willing to bet that the No. 414 and No. 448 teams are going with four tires."

"You'd better be right."

"I'm right. Bring it in, Kent. And watch your speed on pit road."

Thinking of that botched pit stop earlier in the race, Amy chewed her lip. Another misstep like that would be disastrous at this point.

She twisted her hands in her lap, listening to the voices through her headset. Kent was vocally impatient throughout the pit stop, Tobey still reassuring. The stop took just under fourteen seconds, and when Kent reentered the track, he was in eighth place. He wasn't happy about losing those positions, but Tobey insisted they would recover. Four of the drivers ahead of them had gained spots only because they had gambled and hadn't taken the time to change tires. Of the top eight, only Justin Murphy, Kent's dad Dean Grosso and Kent had fresh tires.

They would all see now if that strategy paid off.

Realizing her hands were going numb from the tightness of her grip, she loosened them and pushed herself out of the chair, unable to sit any longer. She wasn't the only one, she noticed with a quick glance around. All of the thousands of spectators in the scattered stands were on their feet, yelling and craning their necks to see the parts of the track ahead of them, checking the large screens to watch the action taking place out of their line of view.

It became evident fairly quickly that Tobey had made the right call. The cars with older tires struggled to hold the track, sliding perilously in the turns.

Justin, Dean and Kent, in that order, advanced steadily on the leading cars, each managing to get around until they were third, fourth and fifth. Will Branch had the lead. Leaning against the railing, Amy tried to mentally push Kent forward. Unfortunately, she had no talent for telekinesis. He lost a position when Rafael O'Bryan went low and slipped between Dean and Kent.

Once again, Kent was shouting in her ears, while Tobey tried to keep him calm and Steve attempted to guide him on a clear path back to the front. Half a lap later, Rafael made a mistake by sliding too far up the track, giving Kent a shot at getting around.

"Low! Low!" Steve shouted.

Kent didn't respond verbally, but Amy watched as his car shot low and forward, leaving Rafael behind him again. She cheered, then urged him on beneath her breath.

A battle was taking place for the lead. Will Branch and Justin Murphy were side by side, their cars inches apart. Dean lurked directly behind them, ready to take advantage if their determination to lead caused either of them to make a reckless error.

Will slipped first. His car fishtailed, and even though he quickly regained control, both Justin and Dean were able to capitalize on that moment of weakness. Justin took the lead. Dean was in second, Kent fourth.

"Come on, Kent, you can do this. Go, go, go," Amy muttered, so focused on the track that she was only marginally aware of Tobey saying much the same things through the radio. There was still a chance for Kent to win, she thought optimistically. And still a chance for something to go wrong, a wary little voice inside her head reminded.

Kent crept up beside Will. The spectators gasped when the cars tapped, causing both drivers to work frantically to maintain control. Kent eased ahead, placing himself in front of Will and into the third position.

Attention turned again to the battle for the lead. With less than half a lap to go, Justin hit a patch of loose gravel. Dean got around him, taking the lead to a roar of cheers and boos from the crowd. Justin recovered in time to hold off Kent's heroic effort to get around him. They crossed the finish line in that order—Dean, then Justin, then Kent, with Will and Rafael rounding out the top five.

Third place. Amy watched team members sharing weary high fives and fist-bumps in the pit. None of them were entirely happy with anything but a win, and all were still smarting over the one botched pit stop. But third place—especially at a road track—wasn't too shabby. Tobey could be justifiably proud of the results of his first race as crew chief.

Kent spoke again through the radio, and Amy could hear the exhaustion in his voice now that the adrenaline was beginning to wane. "Sorry, guys, that was the best I could do. Thanks, everyone."

"You did great, Kent," Tobey assured him. "Third place, man. We gained some points."

"Yeah. You did good, Tobey. And, Steve, tell Dad's spotter congratulations, okay? Dad's gotta be stoked that he won."

Since Dean was spinning smoky donuts on the track even as Kent spoke, Amy figured that was an understatement.

She glanced again at the pit box. Surrounded by reporters, photographers and fans, Tobey climbed down to the ground, settling his Vittle Farms cap more securely on his head and speaking into the microphones shoved into his face. Amy could imagine the questions being asked him. How did he feel after calling his first race? Was he satisfied with the finish? What would he do to prepare for next week? The usual rather clichéd postrace chatter, she thought.

She didn't know what caused him to suddenly turn and look toward the top of the hauler where she stood gazing down at him. Their eyes met across the distance, and she felt her heart trip over a couple of beats. She managed to smile at him and give a congratulatory little wave, which he returned with a nod of his head. And then he turned to walk through the crowd toward his driver, and the oddly intimate exchange was over, leaving Amy to try to regain her breath.

CHAPTER SIX

THERE WASN'T a lot of time after the race for postmortems. Packing up and moving out began immediately after Kent brought the car back to the pit. Already the team was focused on the next race, the next skirmish in the season-long points battle. Discussions about today's race, and decisions about next Sunday's, would begin first thing the next morning back at the shop.

Kent usually took Mondays off unless something came up that required his attendance. Crew chiefs rarely had an entire day off, so Amy expected that Tobey was in his office at his usual early hour, though by mid-morning she hadn't caught sight of him.

As for herself, she was in the habit of going in early on Monday to clear away the messages that had collected during the weekend or writing press releases, and then taking off the occasional Monday afternoon to spend time with Gretchen and Aunt Ellen. She was just wrapping up at around noon when a sound from the doorway made her glance up. Her fingers tightened around the pen she was holding. "Oh. Hi, Tobey."

He leaned against the doorjamb, his shaggy hair

tumbled by his hands, his polo shirt and chinos looking a bit wrinkled, as if he'd already put in a long day. "Hi, Amy. Is this a bad time?"

"No, I was just finishing up here."

"Have you had lunch?"

She shook her head. "Not yet, no."

"I'm in the mood for one of those pulled-pork sandwiches from L and M Barbecue. Would you like to join me?"

She set down her pen. "Just the two of us?"

"Yeah. You like barbecue?"

"As long as it's not too spicy. I have sort of a wimpy mouth."

He chuckled, though his gaze lowered to her lips, making her self-conscious about her own suddenly stiff smile. "Doesn't look wimpy to me," he murmured.

She swallowed, thinking that maybe she should decline the lunch invitation and go home to her family, since something told her he hadn't had strictly business in mind when he asked her to join him.

Had the promotion given him a little more confidence when it came to letting her see his attraction to her? Did he really think she would be more willing to go out with a crew chief than a crew chief's assistant? But she was just as wary about getting involved with him now as she had been before, so his title made absolutely no difference.

"Actually, I planned to eat lunch at home today."

He nodded and straightened away from the doorjamb. "No problem. See you around, Amy."

She really should let him go. He didn't seem annoyed or hurt or even particularly disappointed that she had turned him down. Resigned, perhaps. He probably took the refusal as a message that she wasn't interested in spending time with him outside of work. Maybe he thought it had been worth a shot, but hadn't really expected her to go along. He probably wouldn't ask again.

That possibility made her say impulsively, "Tobey?"

He'd already disappeared from sight. In response to her call, he stuck his head back into the doorway. "Yeah?"

She reached for her bag. "Barbecue sounds really good today. I think I will join you."

He smiled, though his eyes searched her face. "Great. Are you coming back here afterward?"

"No, I'm finished here for the day. We can take my car and I'll drop you off here on my way home after lunch."

He nodded. "Sounds like a plan."

It sounded, she thought somberly, like a mistake waiting to happen. But that didn't stop her from walking out with him.

"SO I OPENED MY bedroom door and there was Gretchen, her little face smeared with red lipstick and blush and eye shadow. She had lipstick in her hair and on her clothes, and makeup all over my pale yellow bedspread and even the beige carpet. The whole room reeked of the very expensive perfume she'd spilled. It took me hours to clean up the mess. And all the time, Aunt Ellen had believed that Gretchen was in her own room, taking a nap. After that, we both learned never to take for granted that Gretchen was where we thought she was."

Laughing, Tobey dragged a seasoned French fry through ketchup on his nearly empty plate, in no hurry to bring their lunch conversation to an end. "How old did you say she was?"

"She had just turned five. That was about three months after Aunt Ellen came to live with us."

"And you were only twenty-one?"

"Twenty-two actually. I was seventeen when Gretchen was born. She was a big surprise for my parents, who hadn't thought they could have any children after me. They were crazy about her. Unfortunately, they only got to enjoy her for four years."

"Does she remember them?"

"Not much. I've tried to keep their memory alive for her, but she was so little when they died in that crash. They'd flown to a lakeside resort to celebrate their twenty-fifth wedding anniversary. I'd offered to watch Gretchen that weekend because they so rarely had time to themselves. They never made it home."

She had spoken matter of factly, but Tobey heard the lingering echoes of grief in her voice. He recognized that poorly hidden pain all too well.

"You said your great-aunt came to live with you and Gretchen," he said, trying to keep the conversation moving without letting it get too sad. "You didn't move in with her?"

"No. We didn't want to uproot Gretchen from the house where she'd lived with Mom and Dad. Aunt Ellen lived in a small rental house, whereas our house was paid for by the insurance settlement, so it made sense for her to be the one to move in. She had taken a medical retirement from working as a middle school librarian and her pension wasn't stretching as far as she'd hoped it would after she bought her medications, so getting rid of her rent payments helped her out a lot. Her health has been pretty good for the past ten years, though she still has to watch her blood pressure very closely."

And Amy probably took on that worry, as well, he figured. Between her responsibilities to her job, her little sister and her great-aunt, he questioned if she ever had any time just for herself. He wondered, for instance, if she might take an evening to go out to eat or to a movie with him—not that he ever had that many free evenings these days.

It wasn't that he was hoping for a long-term relationship with her, he assured himself, trying not to let his old, painful memories ruin his enjoyment of this simple lunch. He just enjoyed spending time with her.

"I've been thinking about your sister wanting to attend a race," he said, reaching for his iced tea. "Michigan is too soon and Bristol's probably not the best venue for her, since it's so hectic and crowded there, usually, and being a night race and all…but how do you think she'd like going out to California at the end of the month with us? I talked to Nick Carmichael—his daughter's about Gretchen's age. She and her mom are going to be in California, and Nick thought Lisa, his daughter, would enjoy having someone to pal around with."

Nick was the jackman, a cheery, burly man who hoisted the nearly forty-pound jack with an ease that left observers shaking their heads in wonder. He'd been with the team for several years and was well liked by his co-workers. Everyone knew he was crazy about his wife and only child and that he made sure they attended four or five races each season so they could spend that time together. Nick had thought it was a great idea to bring Amy's kid sister to a race.

"California?" Amy looked thoughtful. "She would be thrilled, but I hadn't actually thought of taking her that far from home."

He shrugged. "So call it an end-of-summer celebration. School starts right after that weekend, doesn't it?"

She nodded. "Gretchen will be starting high school. Ninth grade."

"I remember. Would your aunt want to come, too?"

"No. Aunt Ellen doesn't like to fly."

"Would she be okay by herself for a weekend?"

"Oh, sure. She'd probably enjoy it, actually."

"Great. The team planes will be full, but I'm sure Kent would be happy to have you and Gretchen on his plane that weekend. And she can share your hotel room, right? I know you'll be busy, so Josh can keep an eye on her when she's not with Nick's daughter—the kid's always yapping at my heels for an assignment. And the family outreach programs will keep her occupied part of the time. So it should all work out fine, don't you think?"

She studied his face across the table. "You've gone to a lot of trouble for this."

Did she honestly think he would sink to using her little sister to gain points with her? "She said she wanted to attend a race. I know school starts soon, so I figured California would be the most convenient for you, even though it is the farthest away. If you'd prefer, we'll set up something later in the season. Richmond, maybe. Or New Hampshire."

"I think she would love to go to California. She's always wanted to take a big trip like that, but I haven't had time to make the arrangements. I've met Nick's wife and daughter, and they're both very nice. You've really thought of everything. Thank you, Tobey."

He nodded. "So, I'll talk to Kent about the trip. I bet he'll get a kick out of the idea. You know how he likes it when families spend the weekends together at the track."

Kent was really into family. His own had spent most of his life at various race venues, since Kent's great-grandfather, Milo, had been one of the early drivers in NASCAR and his father, Dean, was still actively competing. His sister, Sophia, was even seriously dating Justin Murphy—unfortunately one of Kent's biggest competitors and the descendent of a family that had been involved in an off-track feud with Kent's family for a couple of generations.

Kent's cousin, Steve, was equally involved with the sport, making it very much a family affair. Which made it even harder on Kent, of course, that his parents were going through a rough patch now. They had always been such a close family, spending so much time together— as the demands of the sport allowed, of course.

As for Tobey, well, he'd learned the hard way that work and family didn't mix when it came to himself. He seemed to be able to fully commit himself to only one, and when Jenny, his fiancée, had given him an ultimatum, he had chosen racing over her. Only later had he realized the full extent of the sacrifice he had made.

Which didn't mean that other people should have to neglect their families for the sake of the job. "I bet Gretchen will get a kick out of seeing you in your element. Maybe it will help her understand a little what a high-pressure position it can be."

"Maybe it will. I just hope she doesn't keep me from effectively doing my work."

"I wouldn't worry about it. You're the best multitasker I've ever met. And if you want to take an occasional break to spend time with your sister at that one race, everyone will understand."

She smiled. "Gretchen's going to be so excited. I'll tell her as soon as we get an okay from Kent."

"You know he'll agree."

"I'm sure he will. I just don't want to take it for granted."

It occurred to Tobey that in the time he had known Amy, she'd never tried to take advantage of her position in any way. She'd asked for no special favors, no autographs or swag to impress her friends, no race tickets or invitations to exclusive racing events, even though no one would have faulted her for any of those things. She just did her job, working at least as hard as anyone else on the team, making herself invaluable to Kent. And to himself, for that matter, since she had given him a lot of valuable advice on how to deal with the media during the crew-chief changeover.

"Now that that's settled, how about some dessert?" he asked. "The fried apple pies here are the best I've ever tasted."

"I think I'll just have a cup of coffee. But, please, don't let that stop you from having dessert."

They lingered over their coffee and his dessert. He talked her into having a bite of his fried pie and she agreed with a sigh that it really was good. They laughed about something that had happened in the shop that morning, then speculated about the upcoming race at a track where Kent had always performed well. Glancing at his watch, Tobey realized with a start that they'd been there for over two hours and he was due back at the shop.

"You have to get back to work," Amy said, apparently reading his expression. "I'm ready if you are."

"I've had such a nice time I hate to see it end," he confessed, smiling at her across the table. "Maybe we can do this again sometime soon?"

Her hesitation was barely perceptible before she nodded and said, "Sure. Why not?"

She seemed as wary as he was of the bond developing between them. Probably just as well. He motioned for their server. "Lunch is on me today."

"Oh, that's not…"

"Amy," he said with a crooked smile, "I've just got a big raise. Let me spend some of it, okay?"

She laughed softly. "Well, if it means that much to you."

"It does." Having delayed as long as he could, he walked with her toward the cash register where a line of well-fed patrons waited to pay for their meals.

AMY WAS HELPING her great-aunt clean the kitchen after dinner that evening when her cell phone rang. Glancing at the screen, she recognized the number with a little jump of her pulse rate. "It's Tobey," she said, trying to sound nonchalant. "I guess I should take it."

One eyebrow just slightly lifted, Aunt Ellen studied her face. "Of course you should take the call. I can finish up in here. All I have to do is wipe the counters."

Amy lifted her phone to her ear. "Hello?"

"Hi, it's Tobey. I hope I'm not calling at a bad time?"

"No, this is fine."

"Great. I just wanted you to know that I talked with Kent and he said he would be delighted to have you and Gretchen join him on the flight to California. Tanya's going, too, and she's looking forward to meeting your little sister. She called while Kent and I were talking."

"You're sure we won't be intruding?"

"I'm sure. Really, Kent seemed tickled by the idea. He said he owes you a lot more than this, considering how much you've done for him and how much you've had to deal with on his behalf this season."

Feeling her cheeks warm a bit, she replied, "I've done my job."

"And done it well. But Kent's still grateful for the extra steps you've taken. He kind of likes the idea of being Mr. Big Shot and making this big gesture for you and your little sister."

Amy tried to decide if she heard any negative undertones to Tobey's comment, but he seemed to be amused rather than sarcastic. As far as she could tell, Tobey genuinely liked Kent and vice versa, though they were still in the very early stages of forming a strong driver–crew chief bond.

"It's very nice of him," she said. "I'll tell Gretchen tonight."

"So, did you have a nice dinner?"

Was he making small talk? A way to prolong the conversation? Carrying the phone into the empty living room, she settled into a chair as she answered, "Yes. Aunt Ellen baked a chicken and served it with wild rice and glazed carrots."

"Man, that sounds good. I had a package of peanut butter crackers and a candy bar out of the vending machine downstairs."

"Aunt Ellen would be scandalized. Didn't you have time to go find real food?"

"No. We had a minicrisis come up here. Nothing major, just a problem in the fab shop. I took care of it."

"You're still at work?"

"I'll head home in a couple hours."

It was pure impulse that made her say, "Why don't you join us for dinner here Wednesday night? You won't have time to make anything for yourself, but you need something more nourishing than peanut butter crackers and candy the night before you leave for Bristol."

"That's a nice offer…."

"Consider it a thank-you for making the arrangements for Gretchen to attend next week's race."

"I'm the superstitious type, you know. If we do well at the track again this weekend, like we did at Watkins Glen, I might start insisting on having dinner at your house the night before we leave each week."

He was teasing, of course. Tobey was one of the least superstitious of the racing insiders she'd met. So, she laughed and said, "If you win this weekend, consider it a standing invitation."

"You're on. What time Wednesday evening?"

"Six-thirty?"

"I'll be there. Thanks, Amy."

"You're welcome. I'll see you at the shop tomorrow."

She closed her phone a minute later, wondering if she was making a mistake to have him over for dinner again so soon. She tried to think of it as a thank-you gesture for what he'd done on Gretchen's behalf, but she knew better than to even try to convince herself of that.

Standing, she moved toward the kitchen. She'd better tell Aunt Ellen that they were having company for dinner Wednesday. And then she would have the pleasure of inviting Gretchen to fly to California on the reigning NASCAR Sprint Cup Series champion's private airplane.

GRETCHEN WAS AS thrilled as Amy had predicted she would be. "California? Really? Oh, my gosh, and we get to fly on Kent's plane? Wait until Jessica and Emily hear about this. They're going to die!"

"Maybe it won't be quite that drastic," Amy murmured, sharing an ironic look with their great-aunt.

"It's going to be so sweet." Gretchen was all but rubbing her hands together in anticipation. "Jessica's been bragging all summer about the cruise her family went on in June, but that wasn't nearly as cool as this is going to be. Flying on a private plane, hanging out with the drivers… She's going to just die."

"But you won't, of course, stoop to bragging or rubbing in your good fortune in front of your friends," Aunt Ellen said warningly. "Because that would just be tacky."

"Tacky" was about the worst criticism their aunt could make about any behavior, Amy thought with a slight smile. Dressing too revealingly was "tacky." Being too loud or too rowdy in public was "tacky." Shouting into cell phones in nice restaurants, talking in movie theaters, smacking gum, being rude to service workers, letting children run wild—all "tacky," in Aunt Ellen's studied opinion.

"I won't brag," Gretchen promised, though she couldn't quite meet her great-aunt's eyes. "I'm just going to tell them about it."

"Be gracious."

"Yes, ma'am. I'm going to go call Jessica right now." She paused in the doorway, looking at Amy with an expression of dazed wonder. "Tobey really set all this up for me?"

"Yes, he did. He wanted you to see a race this season, and he thought this would be the most exciting one for you."

"Wow. He must really like you, huh?"

Amy lifted an eyebrow. "Sounds to me as though he really likes *you*."

Gretchen laughed knowingly. "That wasn't the way it looked to me. But tell him thanks for me, will you?"

"You can tell him yourself. He's having dinner with us again Wednesday evening." Amy had already informed Aunt Ellen, who had responded with pleasure at having another chance to feed a hungry young man. No shrimp this time, she had added ruefully.

Gretchen bounced twice on her bare feet. "Really? Cool. I think I'll make him a macramé bracelet. If I start it tonight, I'll have it finished in time to give it to him Wednesday. It could be like a good luck charm for the race Saturday night at Bristol, you know? You think he'd like it?"

Gretchen had started making bracelets from hemp cord and glass beads that summer to give her something to do when their great-aunt spent the afternoon knitting and watching TV. Amy had never seen Tobey wear jewelry of any kind, but she figured he wouldn't mind if Gretchen wanted to make him a gift of appreciation. "I'm sure he would like it."

Gretchen was already moving toward the stairs, her voice fading as she talked all the way up to her room. "I'll use blue and red beads, like Kent's team colors. I'll have to guess at his size, of course, but that shouldn't be too hard. Actually, I think I'll make two while I'm at it. One for Tobey and one for Kent, because Kent's going to let us ride on his plane."

"I hope Gretchen doesn't develop an awkward crush on Tobey," Amy said when she was sure her sister was out of hearing range. "That could be uncomfortable."

Aunt Ellen laughed and shook her head. "Sometimes you can be oblivious, Amy. Gretchen is quite obviously hoping that something will happen between *you* and Tobey."

Feeling her cheeks go warm, Amy frowned. "I hope she doesn't say anything embarrassing in front of him."

"Give her a little more credit than that. Besides, she wasn't the only one who thought there might be a little spark between you and Tobey last time he was here."

"Now don't you start. It's bad enough that Gretchen's trying to fix me up. I have more than enough to worry about right now without dealing with a couple of matchmakers. Got that?"

Aunt Ellen only smiled serenely. "I won't say another word about it. Now, I'll just go make a list of what I need to buy at the market tomorrow for the nice meal I'm going to make for your guest."

Left alone in the den, Amy shook her head in exasperation. Her sister was making Tobey a bracelet and her great-aunt was planning a feast for him.

Just what had she gotten herself into when she had impulsively invited him to dinner?

CHAPTER SEVEN

TOBEY RUBBED his thumb absently over a blue bead woven into the hemp bracelet fastened around his right wrist. Gretchen had assured him the bracelet would bring him luck. He could certainly use some of that this weekend.

Everything that could go wrong had since they had arrived in Bristol. With this being a Saturday-night race, everyone's usual schedule was slightly off. Lousy weather threatened, equipment had been misplaced and a stomach ailment was passing among the team, making it doubtful that everyone would be up to full capacity when needed. Tobey had been washing his hands almost obsessively, as had Kent, both of them doing everything within their power to keep from catching the bug.

Mitch, the hauler driver who was responsible for providing a certain number of meals for the team, arranged for a deli to bring in simple food for lunch—turkey sandwiches, bags of chips, fruit and cookies for dessert. Tobey noted that a few of the guys who usually put away huge amounts of food only picked at the sandwiches. Nick even skipped dessert, a sure sign that the sweets-loving jackman wasn't feeling up to par.

Fortunately, practice had gone fairly smoothly, though not as well as either Tobey or Kent would have liked. At least they hadn't done as badly as one of the other drivers, who'd wrecked his car in practice and would have to go to his backup car for qualifying later that afternoon. They had a couple of hours until qualifying started, and Tobey had ordered the entire team to rest as much as possible during that interim. Kent and Tanya had headed for his motor home right after practice, where he would use the time to relax and focus so that he would be fresh and "in the zone" for qualifying.

Tobey intended to use those two hours to go over and over his lists and notes. Both he and Kent had asked Amy to keep this block of time free in their schedules today, knowing they would need to carve out whatever downtime they could during this hectic weekend. Tomorrow's program would start early and wouldn't give them a chance to breathe until after the race ended tomorrow night.

Tobey had been too busy to mingle much with the other crew chiefs at the last two races. Not that anyone had a lot of time for socializing at the tracks; most people just hung out with other members of their own teams during those hectic days. There were certainly strong friendships among those who had been involved with the sport for so many years. After all, they spent a minimum of thirty-eight weekends a year together. Their kids played together. They all understood the unique demands of a life in racing. But when it came right down to it, everyone was there for the win.

In one way or another, Tobey had been involved with NASCAR since he was a teenager. And yet, he didn't know nearly as many people as others who'd been around even fewer years. He was aware that he tended to be the reserved type who put in long hours that left little time for socializing. His face was familiar around the tracks, but that was because he'd usually been at Neil's heels, quietly doing his job—and Neil's, too, for the past couple of months, though he'd tried to make sure few people knew about that. He knew it had been a surprise to everyone when Dawson had put an untried crew chief in Neil's chair only two weeks prior to the race at Watkins Glen, and he knew exactly how closely his performance had been studied.

He'd worked on being more personable. He had taken all of Amy's suggestions to heart, smiling more, finding time to greet people and make eye contact as he rushed from one crisis to the next. Kent was pretty much a master of working a crowd, sharing small talk and handshakes, posing for photos and charming the fans, walking and signing autographs while somehow still focusing on the job. But Kent was raised in this world. Some would say it was in his blood. Tobey knew he would never be that good, but then he didn't have to be. He just had to be pleasant enough so that he wouldn't actually drive away fans.

"Nice jewelry, kid."

The rather mockingly growled comment made Tobey drop his hand to his side. Bubba Rankin, a barrel-chested man in his early fifties with a round, buzz-trimmed head and squinty gray eyes, had approached without Tobey hearing him. The crew chief for Rafael O'Bryan, Bubba wore the purple and white colors of his team, which weren't particularly flattering with his ruddy complexion. Tobey didn't really know Bubba, except in passing, but he'd heard rumors that the other man was more than a little difficult to get along with, especially with people he perceived as serious rivals.

"Hey, Bubba. How's it going?"

"Going good for us. From what I hear, you can't say the same about your team. How many you got hugging toilets now?"

Someone nearby snickered, obviously eavesdropping. Keeping his tone sociable, Tobey replied, "Yeah, we've had a stomach bug passed around, but it seems to be getting better. I think everyone's just about back up to speed now."

He mentally crossed his fingers, hoping that would be true by race time.

"So, what, did you bring some germs with you from the day-care center when Ritter promoted you? What was he thinking, anyway? You even old enough to shave yet, kid?"

A couple of people laughed this time, and Tobey realized that several bystanders had slowed to watch. Probably wondering how "the kid" would handle the not-so-innocuous ribbing from "the old-timer."

"I'm old enough to do the job," he said, wishing he could come up with a wittier retort. Bubba's attitude really annoyed him, especially since he'd had to deal with those sorts of comments before. It wasn't even as if he were the youngest crew chief ever in NASCAR. He just had the misfortune of looking younger than he actually was.

"Think so, eh? Guess we'll see Saturday night. Bristol ain't known for being an easy race to win, even for an experienced team."

"My team has plenty of experience. We managed to win the championship last year. And since we finished ahead of you guys last weekend, I guess we know what we're doing this season, too."

He heard a few barely muffled guffaws, and Bubba obviously heard them, too. The other man's ruddy face flushed even darker and his thick brows drew downward. Yet he made an effort to keep anyone from seeing that Tobey had gotten to him. "Like I said, we'll see."

"Tobey." A soft hand fell lightly on his arm. "Did you forget about the *Sports Illustrated* phone interview this afternoon? You should hurry or you'll be late."

He'd never been so grateful to see Amy. "Okay, I'm coming. Thanks. See you around, Bubba."

"Yeah. See you, kid."

Amy matched her steps to Tobey's as they moved away. "That was starting to look ugly," she said.

"I was handling it. But I've got to admit I was glad to see you," he added.

"Have you been getting a hard time from many people?"

"Oh. You know. Gotta pay my dues. And Neil was a popular guy. Guess it's only natural that some people would blame me for his dismissal. I think Neil and Bubba went drinking together sometimes."

"You're being pretty understanding considering how rude he was to you."

He shrugged. "I'm not trying to win any popularity awards with the other teams. I'm just here to do my job."

"If it makes you feel any better, most of the other teams seem to like what they know of you. You've earned a lot of respect for the graciousness you've shown during the changeover. As for Bubba, well, you handled that situation just fine. You held your temper, but you didn't let him walk all over you. Word will get around about that."

"Let's just hope he doesn't find out that I did the phone interview two hours ago."

She laughed unrepentantly. "Oops. My mistake."

On an impulse, he asked, "Are you busy now?"

"I can take a few minutes. Why?"

"I thought you might like to see my new motor home. It's pretty cool," he added with an attempt at a winning smile. "There was a delay so I didn't get it until this week. I haven't gotten to show it off to anyone but Joey yet."

Her hesitation was barely perceptible. "Okay, sure. I'd love to see it."

With a mental vow that he would be on his best behavior as he gave her the tour, he motioned for her to precede him toward the reserved motor home lot.

TOBEY'S home-away-from-home fit in very well with the other motor homes on the secured Drivers' and

Owners' lot, Amy noted when he pointed it out to her. The outside was dark red and silver with black accent swirls. Three pneumatically powered sections slid out to add space inside. "Very nice."

"Wait until you see the inside." He keyed in a security code on the number pad at the mid-entry door, then stepped aside to allow her to go in ahead of him.

The interior was clean, sparkling—and monochromatic, she noted at once. The flooring from the entry to the back bedroom was beige granite tile. Beige carpeting softened the salon area. The long couch, two recliners, captain's chair/driver's seat and banquette booth were all upholstered in soft-looking beige leather. The table, a built-in desk and the kitchen countertops were made of brown-flecked marble. Even the throw pillows on the couch were patterned in muted beige and brown. There was nothing out of place, no trace of personality that she could see. Of course, Tobey had owned it for only a week, she reminded herself.

"That's a forty-two-inch plasma TV," he said, pointing to the screen suspended above the driver's section. "There's another in the bedroom. And the kitchen…I mean, the galley, is pretty nice, too. See? Microwave/convection oven, side by side refrigerator/freezer, two-burner stove. There's even a dishwasher, a garbage disposal and a stacked washer and dryer. All the luxuries of home."

She couldn't help but be a little amused by the barely suppressed excitement in his voice. He wasn't bragging, she realized. He was just rather in awe that this motor home actually belonged to him. She supposed she couldn't blame him for that. "It's great, Tobey. Really nice."

"It's not as fancy as Kent's, of course," he admitted, "but it will certainly suit my purposes. The last owners took really good care of it. It's like new."

"I know you'll enjoy having a place to escape to whenever you have a few minutes to yourself. And it will certainly save you commuting time at the beginning and end of the days."

"Yeah. That's the best part, really. With the golf cart I've got parked outside, I can be at the garage in two minutes if they need me."

He opened a sliding wood door at the back of the galley. "This is the bedroom," he said with a wave of his hand. "There's a lot of storage and closet space. And a pretty nice-size bathroom with a shower and a skylight."

She peeked into the bedroom, noting that the big bed was covered with a plain brown spread and that the bathroom was appointed with brass, mirrors and the same brown granite used in the front of the motor home. The second TV was mounted high on the opposite wall from the bed, so that Tobey could lie against the pillows and watch programming beamed in from the built-in satellite system.

He was right, of course. Compared to Kent's palatial motor home—and those of many of the other star drivers—this one was actually rather modest. But it was still quite a luxury, and one that served Tobey well. "It looks to me as if you got a real great deal. I bet you're going to enjoy it."

He nodded. "It belonged to an acquaintance of Dawson's, and Dawson knew the guy was looking to upgrade to a newer one. Thanks to Dawson, the whole deal went really smoothly."

She turned to smile at him. "He's a good man to work for, isn't he?"

"The best. He gave Neil a lot more chances to keep his job than most owners would have."

"It's a shame Neil couldn't seem to be satisfied with what he had with the team," she stated, looking around the tidy bedroom.

"Neil can never be satisfied with anything," Tobey agreed somberly. "That's why he's been married three times and engaged a couple more. He's always discontented, always looking for something that he thinks will make him happy. He had this great job, a darned good salary, a strong relationship with Kent, a girlfriend who seemed to suit him well enough—but he still couldn't stay away from the bars and the booze."

She shook her head firmly. "Neil made his choices. And you did everything you could to help him keep his job. So, if you're feeling guilty about anything concerning him, just don't. It's your turn now. Enjoy it."

He nodded, though there was still a hint of shadow in his eyes as he changed the subject. "Can I get you anything? Stan and Margaret, the couple who'll be driving and taking care of the motor home for me, stocked the fridge with sodas and waters and there's a big pitcher of iced tea. I've got some fruit and ice cream and a chocolate cake for snacks. I'd offer to make a pot of coffee, but I make the worst coffee ever. It's been compared unfavorably to lighter fluid."

She laughed. "I make a pretty good pot of coffee, actually, if you'd like some. Just show me where everything is."

"Really? That would be good with the chocolate cake." He looked at the cabinets as if trying to see through the laminated doors. "I don't really know where everything is yet."

Still smiling, she moved past him. "I'll find what I need. You just sit at the table and keep me company."

Rather than moving immediately away, he stood where he was, so that she nearly bumped into him when she stepped closer to the cabinets. Very aware of him standing so close to her, she cleared her throat. "Tobey?"

He reached up to brush a strand of hair away from her cheek. "You look good here," he murmured. "I had a feeling you would."

"Go sit down," she said and knew he could hear the husky tone to her voice. "I'll make the coffee."

The look in his eyes called her a coward, but he merely nodded and moved obediently away, leaving her to search the cabinets with hands that weren't quite steady.

Fortunately, by the time she had located the coffeemaker and supplies, brewed a pot of coffee and served it with two slices of the chocolate cake she found in the fridge, she had regained her equilibrium. Her phone rang only once during that process, but it was a call she handled quickly.

Tobey was back on his good behavior when she slid

into the booth on the other side of the table from him. They talked business as they began to eat—about a couple of appearances Kent had made that morning and a few that were scheduled before the next evening's race, about an ad campaign Kent had agreed to participate in despite his lack of enthusiasm for filming silly TV commercials. About how practice had gone and what Tobey expected from qualifying.

He reached for his coffee cup and her attention was caught by the knotted rope fastened around his right wrist. Gretchen had worked in three beads, two blue with a red bead in the center, and had put it on Tobey's wrist herself when he'd joined them for dinner the night before. He'd seemed to be quite touched by the gift. Amy had wondered at the time if he really was, or if he was just a good actor.

"You don't have to wear that here, you know," she said, reaching out to touch the bracelet. "Gretchen wouldn't know."

"Why wouldn't I wear it? She gave it to me for luck. I can use all the luck I can get this weekend. Besides, Kent's wearing his, too. We both got a kick out of them."

"I know it isn't really your style."

He shrugged, and glanced down at his wrist. "I like it. It was nice of your sister to make them."

"She was so thrilled about the trip to California. She wanted to do something to thank you both for going to the trouble to arrange it for her."

"It's like I told her, I didn't do that much. I just made a couple of phone calls. She's a nice kid, Amy. You and your aunt have done a good job raising her."

He couldn't possibly know how much that compliment meant to her. She had spent so many years agonizing over whether she was a suitable guardian for Gretchen. "Thanks. It isn't fair, of course, that Gretchen had to grow up without our parents. They gave me such a wonderful childhood, and I wish she could have known them longer. I've had to make a real effort not to let myself spoil her in an effort to make up to her what she lost."

Though his expression was sympathetic, he kept his tone even when he said, "I can tell you've struck the right balance. She doesn't seem at all spoiled."

"Yes, well, you've only seen her on her best behavior," Amy admitted wryly. "She can be a pain in the butt when she wants to be."

He laughed. "Well, she is a teenager. I remember my sisters at that age. Man, they grew claws and fangs on a fairly regular basis."

"While you, I'm sure, were a perfect angel."

"You know what they say about preachers' kids, right? Trust me, there's a reason we have such bad reputations."

She laughed, then after a moment, asked, "How old were you when you lost your father?"

His smile faded. "I was fifteen."

"Not much older than Gretchen," she murmured.

"No."

His hand still lay on the table. She reached out to cover it with her own. "I'm sorry."

Lacing his fingers with hers, he met her eyes. "I guess we both know how much it hurts. But I only lost one of my parents. I can't imagine losing both at once."

Her phone buzzed again, and while the sound made her jump, she was almost relieved that the somber mood was broken. "Excuse me," she said, and disentangled their hands so she could take the call.

Tobey nodded and finished his coffee while she dealt with the call, confirming Kent's appearance at a sponsor autograph event first thing the next morning. She glanced at her watch when she disconnected after only a couple of minutes. "I'd better get back to the hauler. I'm sure you have some things to do before qualifying."

"I just wanted to relax for a few minutes before heading back to the garage. I'll walk that way with you."

They cleared away their dishes in the efficient little galley. Tobey was grinning again when they stacked the dishes in the drawer-styled dishwasher. "Cool gadget, huh? Nicer than the one I have in my apartment back home."

"Really?" It occurred to her only then that she hadn't even thought about where he lived. "You have an apartment?"

"Yeah. It seemed like a waste to buy a house where I wouldn't do much more than sleep and shower."

She laughed. "And yet the first thing you bought when you got the promotion was this fancy motor home."

"Secondhand," he reminded her. "But, yeah, I'll probably spend more time in this than I do in my place back home, considering I'm at the shop an average of fourteen hours a day."

"Anyone ever call you a workaholic?"

His smile dimmed, just a bit, but enough to let her

know she'd hit a nerve. "Yeah. A couple of people might have mentioned that."

She patted his arm in a sympathetic gesture. "I've heard it a few times myself."

"Guess we make quite a team, huh?"

She moistened her lips before saying lightly, "Yes, I guess we do."

He was blocking her way to the door, and he didn't seem to be in any hurry to move. She looked up at him with raised eyebrows, wondering if there was anything else he wanted to say.

He seemed to be looking at her mouth. "Remember that kiss for luck at Watkins? It seemed to work, since we finished third."

He'd kissed her cheek before that race, and it had been nearly an hour before her face had stopped tingling, at least in her overactive imagination. She forced a smile. "Probably just a coincidence."

His lips quirked, and now she was staring at his mouth, too. "Only one way to know for certain, don't you think?"

"Um—" What had they been talking about? Oh, yes, luck. "I thought you weren't the superstitious type."

"I could learn to be." He lowered his head and brushed his lips lightly against her cheek.

Oh, the heck with it. "That only got us third place," she said, catching hold of his shirt. "Let's go for the pole today."

He grinned his approval just before she pressed her mouth to his.

By the time the kiss ended, neither one of them was smiling. They were dazed, breathless, and in Amy's case, more than a little rattled. This thing between them, whatever it was, was getting out of control fast. All the legitimate reasons she'd had for not wanting to get too close to him in the first place were still swirling through her mind, whispering of certain regret.

And yet…kissing Tobey had quite possibly been the most exhilarating experience of her life.

"I'll walk you back," he said, and his voice was little more than a husky growl, proving that he'd been as affected by the kiss as she had.

She got the impression that he was no more ready than she was to talk about that explosive kiss just yet. There were still some things that worried her about Tobey, a feeling that he wasn't letting her get as close to him as she would like, even as he sent her pretty clear signals that he wanted to take their friendship further. Natural reserve? Or a disturbing tendency toward secrecy? She didn't know him well enough to tell yet.

She doubted that she was the only one who was thinking about what a mistake it could be for the crew chief and the PR rep to get personally involved. But from the way his hand rested at the small of her back as he escorted her out of his motor home, she suspected she wasn't the only one wondering if it was too late to stop it now.

CHAPTER EIGHT

TOBEY, KENT, Tanya, Dawson and Amy watched the coverage of the final ten qualifying attempts from the hauler lounge. It was always a bit nerve-racking after Kent's run. Alone on the track, he ran the fastest two laps he could manage, and from then on it was out of his hands.

He'd left the track knowing he had the fastest time of the day, but he'd also known any of the ten cars scheduled to follow him could post better times, pushing him farther and farther back in the field. They all groaned when Justin Murphy's qualifying lap was just a split second faster than Kent's, giving him the pole, but everyone breathed a big sigh of relief when Kent's speed wasn't beaten by anyone else that afternoon. Tanya leaned over to give him a kiss, telling him she was proud of how well he had done considering the rough start they'd had that day.

"Second place." Dawson thumped Kent's shoulder, then patted Tobey's back. "Not too shabby, boys."

It wasn't as satisfying for any of them as taking the pole would have been, but no one was complaining, least of all Tobey. "Thanks, sir. Kent ran a heck of a lap out there. Stayed right in the groove."

Kent reached out to bump Tobey's knuckles with his own. "The car was handling real good today. Little squirrelly in Turn Two, but other than that, I've got no complaints."

"We'll keep an eye on that," Tobey promised. It wouldn't be normal if the driver didn't have some sort of complaint about the car, he thought in resignation. He and the team could give Kent the perfect machine and he'd still find something to fret about.

Dawson cleared his throat. "I just want you to know, Tobey, that I've been pleased at how smoothly the changeover has been going. It's been a tough time for all of us, but you're handling it very well. Whatever you've been doing to get prepared, you keep it up, you hear?"

Tobey very deliberately avoided Amy's eyes, though he suspected she was just as carefully not looking at him. "Yes, sir. I'll do that."

He glanced at Kent, who seemed to be studying him carefully, as if Kent had heard something in Tobey's voice that puzzled him. Tobey cleared his throat. "Of course I can't take all the credit. Everyone's been working hard the past few weeks."

"Nobody giving you any trouble?" Dawson asked.

"Nothing I can't handle," Tobey replied evenly. He would keep any problems to himself as much as possible, giving no one any reason to worry that he couldn't effectively lead his team. Truth be told, there were a couple of guys who weren't happy that Tobey had replaced Neil and they'd let that dissatisfaction show in ways both subtle and overt, but he didn't need the owner stepping in to smooth things over for him. If he couldn't deal with the occasional friction and conflict, he didn't deserve to be a crew chief.

"What's that thing you're wearing on your arm, there, Tobey?" Dawson asked. "I don't think I've seen you wear it before."

Tobey glanced down at his wrist, which was bared by his short-sleeve team polo shirt. "It's a good-luck charm from Amy's little sister, Gretchen. Got the team colors worked into it. She thought we could use a little extra fortune this weekend."

Kent pulled back the sleeve of his long-sleeve uniform. "She made me one, too. Maybe we can thank her for our second-place qualifying, considering how lousy our luck seemed to be earlier today."

Dawson chuckled, not seeming to find anything odd in the fact that Amy's sister had made gifts for Tobey and Kent. "Wasn't that nice of her? How old is your little sister now, Amy?"

"She's fourteen."

"Challenging age. But I'm sure she's delightful."

"You'll meet her yourself next weekend," Kent announced. "Amy's bringing Gretchen to the race in California. She's going to hang out some with Nick's daughter."

"Well, isn't that nice? I've met Lisa. Sweet girl. You be sure and introduce me to your sister, Amy."

"I will," Amy promised, but Tobey thought she looked a bit uncomfortable at having her personal life intrude into her professional role.

Wonder how she would feel if anyone here knew just how personal their own professional relationship had gotten? Not that he intended to kiss and tell, of course. Even if it happened again. And if it were up to him—it would happen again.

He wondered how Amy would feel about *that*.

Kent glanced at his watch. "Guess we'd better get a move on," he said to Tanya. "We've got another half a dozen things scheduled before that sponsor party tonight."

"You're sure I have to go to that thing?" Tobey asked Amy wistfully. "I'm really not a party kind of guy."

"You are now," she answered him relentlessly. "The sponsor wants their driver and crew chief to show up and charm the guests, so that's what they'll get."

"It's not as if you'll be alone," Tanya assured him, taking pity on him. "Kent, Amy and I will be there. All you have to do is sign some autographs, pose for a few dozen pictures with guests, maybe dance a couple of times, and then you can make your escape by saying you need to rest up for the big day tomorrow."

Tobey groaned. "Nobody said anything about dancing."

Kent spared him no pity. "It's a fancy prerace party for Vittle Farms' well-connected associates, Harris. There will be dancing."

"I'm a lousy dancer."

"I'll dance with you," Tanya volunteered. "And so will Amy. Won't you, Amy?"

"As long as you promise not to stomp on my toes," she teased. "I'll be wearing sandals."

The thought of dancing with Amy made the idea of the party a little more inviting. "I'll try not to break any bones."

"That would be greatly appreciated."

Dawson laughed. "I'm leaving the late-night parties to you young'uns. Anna and I will be in bed by then. But I'll be around bright and early tomorrow, so don't you boys overdo it tonight."

"Amy and I will make sure they behave themselves," Tanya said with an easy laugh.

"Right," Amy murmured wryly. "As though either of them would put anything ahead of racing."

"Well, maybe just one or two things," Kent said, wrapping an arm around his fiancée and dropping a kiss on her hair.

An old pain shot through Tobey's heart, making it hard for him to hold on to his own smile. Wonder how they would all feel if they knew that his obsession with racing had caused him to break the heart of a very sweet, slightly needy young woman? And that he would always secretly wonder if his selfish pursuit of his career had cost the life of his fiancée—and ended what might have been his only chance at having a family of his own?

He moved abruptly toward the door. "I've got to get to the garage. I'll see you guys later."

He couldn't look at Amy as he walked out.

AMY HADN'T BEEN on a double date in years. She barely had time for regular dates. Not that the sponsor party that evening could be considered a date, either double or otherwise. She just happened to be in attendance with Tobey, Tanya and Kent. Kent liked having her around in case any PR issues came up, and Tobey hadn't wanted to be a third wheel at Kent and Tanya's side, so her presence was required as part of her job.

None of which explained, of course, why she had spent almost twice as much time as usual doing her hair and makeup for this event and wondering if she'd brought the right dress to wear. She had finally made herself stop obsessing and had convinced herself that the simple but eye-catching red sheath was both flattering and appropriate. Red was one of Kent's colors, and happened to look good on her. And if she hoped Tobey noticed…well, she was only human.

She'd been inordinately pleased when Tobey had taken one look at her and said simply, "Wow."

Speaking of Tobey, she thought, glancing at him as he chatted with a Vittle Farms' vice president, he looked pretty darned good himself. He wore a dark suit with a white shirt and a red-and-blue-patterned tie. He'd found time to have his hair trimmed and while she privately liked it shaggy and disheveled, she had to admit the tidy, professional look suited him, too.

Despite his expressed concerns about mingling in this social setting, he'd handled the first twenty minutes just fine. Of course, so far the conversation had all been pretty much about business, centering around the satisfactory qualifying run that afternoon, about the race tomorrow, about the points standing and some new rules NASCAR had recently implemented. He was comfortable enough talking about racing.

She could tell when he'd said all he could on that subject to the vice president. He started looking a little tense, as if searching his mind for some new topic. She moved to his side. "Tobey, there's someone who would love to meet you. Do you mind if I steal him away, Carl?"

Having successfully extricated him, she towed him across the room.

"Thanks," he stated. "I was out of small talk."

"You're doing fine."

"Is there really someone who wants to meet me or was that a mercy rescue?"

"Both." She paused in front of an older woman with dyed red hair and a too-young black dress. "Mrs. Kelley, I promised to introduce you to Kent's new crew chief. This is Tobey Harris. Tobey, Mrs. Kelley's father was one of the original partners in Vittle Farms."

"It's a pleasure to meet you, ma'am."

"Well, look at you. Aren't you handsome?" Mrs. Kelley, whom Amy estimated to be somewhere in her late seventies, took hold of Tobey's arm and gazed up at him with a smile that was openly flirtatious. "How old are you, Tobey?"

It was to his credit that he kept smiling. "I'm twenty-eight."

She nodded. "Plenty old enough to know what you're doing, eh? And not just in the pits, isn't that right?"

His lips twitched. "Yes, ma'am."

"You going to win this championship thing this year?"

"We're going to try."

She thumped his arm. "That's the spirit. My uncle used to race cars back in the forties. They called him 'Catch-Me' Kelley. He might have been one of the early NASCAR stars himself, but my aunt made him quit racing when their first child was born. Racing wasn't as safe back then, you know, and she didn't want to risk raising my cousins by herself. I don't think my uncle ever quite forgave himself for letting that dream go so easily, though. There's a lesson to you kids. Don't be afraid to go after your dreams, you hear?"

"We're both doing exactly that, Mrs. Kelley," Amy assured her after sharing a quick, amused glance with Tobey.

"Glad to hear it."

Tobey seemed fascinated by the older woman. "What about you, ma'am? Did you go after your dreams?"

She gave him a dimpled smile that hinted of the mischievous young woman she had once been. "I went after plenty of them. Caught me a few, too."

He laughed. "Bet you've got some great stories to tell."

She patted his arm again. "Come visit me sometime and I'll share a few with you."

"I just might take you up on that."

"Mother Kelley." A tall, very slender woman with diamonds at her ears and throat and an unnaturally smooth forehead appeared to take Mrs. Kelley's arm. "I wondered where you'd gotten off to. Come sit down and let me get you something to eat."

"I'm coming, Belinda. My daughter-in-law," she

added in a low voice to Amy and Tobey. "Her dream was to marry well. She did. Twice."

Tobey was laughing again when Belinda towed Mrs. Kelley away after exchanging polite nods with them. "I don't think Belinda cares for racing people," Tobey murmured to Amy when the duo was out of hearing range.

"She's the kind who prefers politicians and trendy intellectuals," Amy whispered back. And then winced. "Ouch, that sounded catty. I shouldn't make snap judgments on someone I've only met a couple of times."

He shrugged. "Sometimes that's all it takes. You might have noticed I don't have a lot of use for polite little social games."

"Yes, well, it's part of your job now," she reminded him.

Kent and Tanya approached just in time to hear that last exchange. Kent looked dashing, as always, in his tailored suit and expensive tie, and Tanya glowed in a buttercup-yellow strapless dress. NASCAR's sweethearts, as they'd been referred to many times, were in fine form tonight. Because her own career kept her so busy, Tanya wasn't always able to join Kent at the tracks, but she made an effort to be with him as often as possible. Kent always looked so happy to have her nearby.

"Don't get my dad and great-grandfather started on the PR part of modern racing," Kent said, keeping his voice just low enough for the four of them to hear. "Especially Milo," he added, referring to his legendary great-grandfather, who'd been one of the earliest competitors in NASCAR. "He said he never even owned a tie back when he was racing, and the only parties he went to involved barbecues and beer kegs. He makes fun of me every time he opens a magazine and sees my face selling watches and cologne and breakfast cereal."

"I've seen your grandfather in a tuxedo, and I've watched him work a society event like an old politician," Amy reminded Kent with a wry smile. "He just likes to pretend to be a good old boy from the backwoods."

"That's because he does it so well," Tanya agreed with a smile. "I'm starving, you guys. You think we've worked the room enough to justify sitting down for a few minutes with some food?"

"Of course. But you should sit at a table with some of your fans, rather than with Tobey and me," Amy instructed Kent. "You don't want to look standoffish."

"No," Kent said with a sigh. "We wouldn't want that."

"Kent looks tired," Amy fretted to Tobey when Kent and Tanya moved toward the loaded food tables. "He should make his excuses soon and go get some rest, considering the schedule he has tomorrow."

"You're the one who lined up that schedule," Tobey reminded her. "Don't worry, he'll be fine. He's just drained from practice and qualifying."

Kent wasn't the only one who looked tired, she thought, studying the slight shadows beneath Tobey's eyes. "You know, I could use something to eat, myself," she said. "How about you?"

"Yeah. I've been eyeing those little chicken wings. And if I'm not mistaken, those are cheesecake bites on the dessert table."

A few minutes later, they carried their filled plates to a large round table for eight at which only two couples were seated. Amy and Tobey introduced themselves and took two of the empty chairs.

Tobey was immediately inundated with the usual eager questions. He managed to answer them all while still putting away the chicken wings, some marinated asparagus spears, stuffed mushrooms and bruschetta with tomato and basil. Amy snacked on shrimp cocktail, tiny crab cakes and salmon and prosciutto rolls. They had both selected a few treats from the dessert table. Tobey had a glass of wine with his food; Amy washed hers down with coffee, choosing decaf since it was getting late.

She had discreetly watched Tobey fill his plate, noting that he was very careful to stay away from anything that might contain shellfish. She wondered if he'd ever had a life-threatening experience with his food allergy. There were still so many things she wanted to know about him. Which made her think of that too-guarded reticence of his again, though she quickly pushed the uncomfortable thought to the back of her mind. Tobey would tell her more as they spent more time together, she decided. She couldn't imagine that he was hiding anything too troublesome.

He turned to her as if he knew somehow that she'd been thinking of him. "I believe I'll have a cup of coffee to go with my sweets. Can I get you anything else?"

"No, I'm fine, thanks."

He glanced around the table. "Anyone else need anything?"

When no one did, he nodded and moved away, saying he would be right back.

"He is so cute," one of the women at the table stage-whispered to Amy, causing her friend to giggle and the two men to roll their eyes. "I just love the gorgeous, shy types."

"Hey," her husband protested.

The woman—whose name Amy thought was Karen—giggled again and patted her husband's arm. "That's what attracted me to you, of course," she assured him. "I'm just saying."

Marginally appeased, he filled his mouth with a big bite of a chocolate-dipped strawberry while she turned back to Amy. "So, are the two of you—?"

Her husband made a funny, beeping sound and Karen grinned. "He does that when he thinks I'm getting too nosey," she confided to Amy. "He says I get too personal sometimes, but I told him all anyone has to do is tell me they prefer not to answer when I ask perfectly innocent questions. So are you and Tobey an item? You don't mind my asking, do you?"

Following the other woman's rambling with an effort, Amy laughed a little nervously. "Um, no, I don't mind your asking, but Tobey and I are just friends and associates. Now that he's Kent's crew chief, we all spend a lot of time together. It takes quite a few people to keep a top-level NASCAR team running smoothly."

By the time Tobey returned with his coffee, Amy had skillfully redirected the conversation back to racing, impressing her listeners with details about the number and variety of people employed on both a full-time and part-time basis in the offices, shops and garages. One of the men asked Tobey to explain something about the number of pit crew members allowed over the wall during a pit stop, and Amy could relax again as everyone's attention turned away from personal questions.

Music had been playing through a hidden sound system until that point in the gathering. The official host of the party climbed onto a small stage then to thank Kent and Tobey again for attending and to give away door prizes from tickets the guests had purchased as they'd arrived. The proceeds from the raffle were to be donated to a children's charity supported by both Vittle Farms and Maximus Motorsports.

Karen squealed when she won a basket filled with Kent Grosso licensed merchandise—a T-shirt, cap, water bottle, coffee mug and die-cast car. "Do you think he'd autograph these things for me?" she asked Amy and Tobey, both of whom assured her that Kent would be delighted to do so.

After the other prizes—including a tour of the garage, pits and hauler before tomorrow's race—were distributed with rounds of applause, the host introduced a local band who would play for the next hour. He encouraged everyone to dance or just to stay and listen.

Some of the guests made their way to the exits then, Amy noted, but quite a few stayed, eager to keep partying. She knew there were prerace parties all over the area that evening, and that others would go on well into the night in the campgrounds both within and around the track. For most fans, parties and festivities were as much a part of a race weekend as the event itself.

The two other couples from their table moved to the dance floor. Kent and Tanya rejoined Amy and Tobey then, Tanya assuring them that she felt much better now that she'd had a chance to eat.

"We're not going to stay much longer," Kent said. "Have to get an early start in the morning."

"But you're going to dance with me first," Tanya reminded him, glancing eagerly toward the dance floor. "It seems like forever since we've had a chance to dance together."

Kent smiled indulgently. "Okay, one dance."

"Three."

"Two."

"Deal." Laughing, Tanya took his arm and playfully towed him toward the floor.

"You said you would dance with me," Tobey reminded Amy. "As long as I promised not to crush your toes."

She smiled. "I haven't forgotten. And I'm holding you to that promise."

Taking her hand, he led her to the dance floor.

TOBEY DROVE Amy back to her hotel. The country club was some distance away from where she was staying, and there was quite a bit of race-crowd traffic, so it took a while to get there.

He didn't mind. He enjoyed spending the extra time alone with her.

"Now admit it," she said as they put the country club behind them. "The party wasn't as bad as you thought it would be."

"No," he acknowledged. "It wasn't bad."

Because Amy had been there. And because she had danced with him. And because she had felt so very good in his arms. None of which he thought it prudent to add at the moment.

She laughed softly and for a moment, he wondered if he had somehow given away his thoughts. "Admit it, you'd still rather be in the garage than at a party."

"For the most part, yes." Unless, of course, said party gave him another chance to wrap his arms around Amy.

No, what was he thinking? He gave his head an impatient little shake. Of course he would rather be in the garage. That was where he would always be happiest.

Sighing lightly, she nestled more snugly into her seat. "It's been a long day."

"I'm sure you're tired. I hope you can get some rest tonight."

She turned her head against the back of the seat to smile at him. "You, too. I guess you'll find out tonight if your motor home is worth the expense, hmm?"

He chuckled. "Yeah, I guess. I know it gets pretty loud in the fan campgrounds, but I hope it'll be a little quieter in the drivers' and owners' lot. I could use a solid five hours of sleep."

Because it made him suddenly uncomfortable to be talking about sleeping arrangements with her, he changed the subject. "Do you like all the traveling that goes with your job? Sleeping in hotels? Being away from home so much?"

"There are downsides, of course, to being on the road so much, but for the most part I enjoy traveling. Not that I see a lot of the different places we go to, because we stay so busy while we're there. Still, I like being part of the team, you know? Everyone working together toward one goal, and me being an integral part of that. I know that sounds kind of hokey."

"No, it doesn't. I think everyone on the team would agree with you."

"What about you? Do you like traveling?"

"I like racing. I go where the tracks are."

She laughed a little at his matter-of-fact response. "Of course."

"All this traveling is hard on a social life, though," he said, wondering how to pursue that topic without getting too personal. "Especially since it's typically weekends when we're out of town."

She shrugged. "I think we talked about this once before, on Kent's plane. I don't have much of a social life outside of the job, but that's not really a problem for me at this point in my life."

"Nobody special back home?"

"No. I've dated some, of course, but between my job commitments and my responsibilities to Gretchen and Aunt Ellen, not many guys are patient enough to hang around for long. I was dating someone pretty seriously when my parents died—seriously enough that we'd started talking marriage—but he wasn't interested in raising Gretchen. He couldn't understand why I'd want to 'saddle myself with a toddler,' as he phrased it, rather than giving her to someone else to raise."

Tobey raised an eyebrow. "He thought you could just give away your little sister?"

"To give him credit, Brandon was pretty young. Only twenty-two, barely out of his parents' house himself. He just assumed there were other adults who could take care of Gretchen for me. When Aunt Ellen offered to move in, he thought I would let her take over Gretchen's care full-time. It didn't take him long to realize that I took my position as her guardian very seriously. Aunt Ellen took care of the household and watched Gretchen while I worked, but I was ultimately responsible for Gretchen's welfare, and Aunt Ellen never disputed that. Brandon drifted away when the reality of the situation became too much for him."

"Some guys just aren't cut out for family life," Tobey muttered, shifting uncomfortably in his seat.

"The last I heard, Brandon and his wife have two kids under five," she said, and he could tell that she was making an effort to try not to let him see that it still stung a bit. She probably didn't even want to believe that herself. Had probably convinced herself that she was long over her ex-boyfriend and the heartache he'd caused her.

"I'm sure he's a good husband and father," she added lightly. "He just wasn't ready for it back then, especially when it came to raising someone else's child."

"You're being very generous," he said. He wondered

what she would say if she had any idea how much he was reading into what little she'd said.

"I didn't want you to think he was a bad guy. He wasn't. Just immature. He didn't leave me with a bitter outlook, but I did learn to make it clear in all my future relationships that Gretchen would always come first with me. And then I got busy with my career, working toward becoming a full-time PR rep, and it just seemed easier not to get too involved. I still go out, but I haven't been looking for anything more than an occasional evening with a friend, you know?"

"I know exactly," he said, rather relieved to hear her describe precisely what he sought in his own limited social life. So maybe he didn't have to work quite so hard to fight his attraction to Amy, after all. As long as she wanted nothing more than a good time while it lasted, there was no reason they couldn't enjoy each other's company.

He had grown quite skilled at ending his temporary liaisons on a pleasant note, and he was still friendly enough with most of the women he'd dated during the past few years. He imagined that he and Amy could remain friendly associates when the time came that they mutually agreed to move on. Assuming they developed anything to move on from, of course.

So, while he wasn't going to rush into anything with her, he wasn't going to push her away, either. He liked her. He liked her family. A guy could always use some new friends. And since neither of them was looking for more than that, there was no reason not to enjoy it, right?

Or maybe he was only rationalizing something he wanted despite the risks, a nagging little voice inside him whispered.

Ignoring any misgivings, he turned the car into the parking lot of Amy's hotel. "I'll walk you up to your room."

"You don't have to do that. You're tired. I'm sure you'd like to get back to your own place."

"My mother would have my hide if she found out I let a lady walk through a hotel parking lot by herself," he intoned solemnly, making Amy giggle.

"This lady has walked through plenty of hotel parking lots alone," she assured him, and then laughed again. "Oh, ouch, that makes me sound a bit shady, doesn't it?"

"Fortunately, I know what you meant." It was a nice evening for being outside. The heat of the summer day had dissipated in the night breeze, leaving the temperature just warm enough to be comfortable. Only a few people were out that late, so it was pleasantly quiet, giving them the illusion of solitude.

He placed a hand lightly at the small of Amy's back as he walked her through the lobby to the bank of elevators. It wasn't that she needed assistance; he just liked touching her. It pleased him that she made no effort to break the contact.

Her room was on the second floor. No one else was in the hallway when they stepped out of the elevator, though he could hear muted voices and television sounds as they passed the numbered, green-painted doors. Amy stopped in front of the last door on the right and slipped her key card into the reader. When the light turned green, she opened the door, then turned to face him from the doorway. "Your mother would be glad to know that you've seen me safely to my room."

Chuckling, he lifted a hand to her face, tracing her lower lip with his fingertip. "I don't really want to talk about my mother just now."

"Oh?" Her eyes were speculative as she smiled up at him. "What do you want to talk about?"

Lowering his head, he murmured, "I don't want to talk at all."

His lips touched hers, lightly, giving her every chance to draw back if she wanted. For a fraction of a second, she hesitated, and he wondered if she was going to do just that. But then her lips parted beneath his, and she leaned into him, resting her hand on his chest and kissing him back with enough heat to make his toes curl in his uncomfortable, wing-tip dress shoes.

He wrapped his arms around her and pulled her closer, loving the way she felt against him. He was entirely too aware of the door that stood so invitingly ajar. It would take only a couple of steps for them to be inside that room with the door closed and locked behind them.

He told himself it was a good thing when Amy pressed against his chest to bring the kiss to an end without either of them taking those steps. They didn't want to take this too fast. If anything happened, it would develop naturally. Casually.

"Good night, Tobey," she said, moving backward with one hand poised to close the door between them.

"I'll see you tomorrow." And because knowing he would made him happy, even as his body protested the abrupt end to those arousing embraces, he found himself humming beneath his breath as he walked back down to his car.

CHAPTER NINE

THE CONCLUSION of the Saturday-night race was a nail-
biter, just the way the fans liked their races to end.
Colorful cars gleamed in the bright, artificial lights, the
drivers sped around the track, fighting for positions,
struggling to stay off the wall and avoid the dreaded
"Bristol stripes" down the sides of their cars. The action
was fast and furious, with several spectacular crashes
that Kent barely avoided.

Amy found herself watching through her fingers,
holding her breath until she realized she was becoming
light-headed. Only then did she drag in oxygen,
ordering herself to relax. She didn't know why she was
suddenly so nervous; it wasn't as if every race this
season hadn't been important. But for some reason, she
really wanted Kent to win this one.

What bothered her most was that she didn't know if
she wanted that win more for Kent or for Tobey.

Unable to wait in the hauler, she stood by the war
wagon as the race drew to a finish. The noise was deafening, but she didn't bother with a headset at that point.
The whole area was crowded with team members,

reporters, security, track officials and other spectators, and Amy was jostled more than once, but she was accustomed to that, too. Her attention was focused solely on the action on the track, as was everyone else's.

It came down to a melee between Kent, Rafael O'Bryan and Will Branch. The three drivers swapped leads several times, occasionally making daring, side-by-side moves that drew loud gasps from the riveted crowd.

Kent's team lined up at the pit wall, shouting encouragement for their driver. Though she couldn't hear him, Amy knew Tobey was urging Kent on, trying to keep him calm and focused while still fired up for the win. Will made a mistake coming out of Turn Four, letting his car drift dangerously high on the track toward the wall. Even though Will recovered quickly, his mistake had cost him. Kent and Rafael now battled for the lead, leaving Will too far behind to catch them.

With three laps to go, Rafael's car started showing the effects of the hard racing. His tires were shot, someone said within Amy's hearing, and she saw Kent's team start to celebrate as Kent drew steadily ahead. Though she worried about last-minute disasters—being the type who never celebrated until the checkered flag flew—she allowed herself to relax just a little and glance up at Tobey instead of at the track. The air of intense satisfaction she saw on him confirmed that he, too, thought they had the race won. Minutes later, his confidence was validated.

Kent won the race.

Pandemonium broke out in the pit. While fireworks

exploded in the sky overhead, Kent's team members whooped and celebrated, surging over the wall to line the track and cheer their driver. Tobey's assistant, Josh Peeples, happened to be standing near Amy; he grabbed her in an enthusiastic hug before moving on to celebrate with his other teammates, leaving her laughing.

On the war wagon, Tobey high-fived and fist-bumped his associates, then jumped down to be surrounded by reporters and well-wishers. He shouted a few responses to questions thrown at him from all sides, but he didn't stop moving. Amy assumed he was headed for Victory Lane with the rest of the team, but he paused to pull her into his arms. "We did it," he said into her ear, his voice shaking a little. "We won."

Touched by that evidence of how very much this meant to him, she smiled mistily as she drew back to look up at him. "I had no doubt that you could."

Something about his expression told her that he would have kissed her then, had they not been in such a public place. The hug would not attract any particular notice, since everyone on Kent's team was hugging and celebrating just then, but a kiss would definitely raise eyebrows. So Tobey released her and turned to shake someone else's hand.

Oddly enough, Amy almost felt as if they had shared a kiss, anyway.

The celebration continued in Victory Lane. Amy watched as Kent planted a joyfully passionate kiss on Tanya, and then exchanged a victorious hug with Dawson and the various Grosso family members there to celebrate with him. He and Tobey hugged, too, and she was pleased to see that it looked heartfelt. It would take more than one win for Tobey to earn his team's unquestioning trust, which he knew as well as she did, but it was a great start.

As for the way *she* felt about Tobey…well, she'd spent several sleepless hours last night trying to decide just that. She still hadn't come up with an answer. She knew only that she wouldn't fight him off if he wanted to kiss her again.

"TOBEY'S SUCH a nice young man. I'm glad you invited him to come with us today. He seems to be having a good time."

"We all needed this nice break today." Sitting on a hand-pieced quilt spread on a patch of thick, green grass, Amy wrapped her arms around her knees. Her sleeveless top and denim shorts kept her cool, despite the heat of the afternoon. She'd kicked her sandals aside, so that her bare toes, with the frivolous coat of pink polish she'd applied that morning, were free to curl into the soft quilt.

A warm breeze teased a strand of hair into her eyes, but she was too lazy to reach up and tuck it back. Aunt Ellen sat in a folding canvas chair nearby with her knitting in her lap, her needles making a soothing clicking sound just audible to Amy over the other noises surrounding them.

The park was moderately crowded on this perfect summer Sunday afternoon, but not so much that they hadn't been able to find a cozy spot for a picnic. The remains of that casual meal of sandwiches, raw veggies and homemade cookies were stashed in a basket near where Amy sat. A few yards ahead of her, Gretchen and Tobey played a spirited game of Frisbee.

Amy noted that Tobey was starting to wilt a bit. As young as he was, he was still twice Gretchen's age. He was probably feeling it just then, she thought, watching him stretch out nearly full-length to catch a disk thrown over his head. He was going to regret that move tomorrow.

It had been Gretchen who had begged Amy to invite Tobey on the picnic they'd planned on Amy's rare Sunday at home. After all, Gretchen had insisted, Tobey rarely had a day off, either. He'd probably enjoy spending this one having fun instead of working.

Though Amy had warned Gretchen that Tobey might well have other plans, she'd allowed herself to be persuaded to call him as soon as she got home. Agreeing to meet them at the park, he had accepted the invitation without even hesitating, seemingly delighted that he'd been included. Aunt Ellen had immediately doubled the amount of food she'd prepared to bring.

He plopped down suddenly onto the quilt beside her, his hair mussed and his face flushed and generally looking more delicious than anything found in a picnic basket. "Your sister just killed me," he announced, one hand on his chest over the Kent Grosso T-shirt he wore with khaki cargo shorts.

"You don't look bad for a dead man," she teased him—and wasn't *that* an understatement?

"Thanks. I guess."

"Want something cold to drink?"

"Yes, please."

She reached into the cooler on her other side and pulled out a canned lemonade. "Will this do?"

"Perfectly. Thanks."

Barely winded, Gretchen waved toward a stand of trees on the other side of the stretch of grass where she and Tobey had played. "Aunt Ellen, you want to walk on the nature path with me?"

Aunt Ellen set her knitting aside. "I'll come with you, but remember that I can't walk as quickly as you do."

"Watch your steps, Aunt Ellen," Amy advised. "You don't want to fall."

Her great-aunt rolled her eyes. "I think I can handle a little stroll on a walking path."

"Of course you can. Sorry." Amy waited until Ellen and Gretchen had moved a few feet away, then added to Tobey, "She fell last spring and badly sprained her left wrist. I've worried about her falling again ever since. It annoys her no end."

Stretching his long legs out in front of him, his ankles comfortably crossed, Tobey said, "I don't blame you for worrying, or her for being annoyed by it."

She smiled. "Nice, noncommittal reply."

"I don't want to risk making Aunt Ellen mad. Not as long as she keeps making me food. Any more of those cookies?"

Amused by how easily he'd taken to saying "Aunt Ellen," just like almost everyone else who knew her, she handed him another peanut butter cookie. He washed it down with swigs of the lemonade. "I'm glad you invited me today," he said, wiping his mouth on a paper napkin. "I can't remember the last time I went on a picnic."

"I wasn't sure if you'd want to just crash at your place today, considering how hectic the last couple of days were."

At least the night race had been held at a track that wasn't too far from their home, she thought, opening a bottled water for herself. Bristol was just a little over three hours away by car. Which was convenient for everyone on the team, considering the long trip to California for the upcoming race.

"No, it's nice to have something to do besides watch TV or work, which is what I usually do when we're not at a track."

She studied him through her lashes. "That sounds a little…"

"Dull? Sad?" He chuckled. "It's not quite as bad as it sounded. I've got friends I hang out with—Joey and a couple other guys. We get together for pick-up basketball games sometimes. Do a little fishing. I just didn't happen to have any plans for today."

She reached over to touch the bracelet he wore on his right arm. "It pleased Gretchen that you wore this today."

"I told her I'm not taking it off. After the weekend we had, I think it really might be lucky."

Laughing, she shook her head. "I'm beginning to think you're a little superstitious, despite your denials."

"Maybe we all are, a little bit. How about you, Amy? Is there anything you do for luck?"

If truth be told, she was a bit superstitious about examining moments of contentment too closely. Maybe because she knew how ephemeral happiness could be. "I'm sure I have my quirks," she said lightly.

Tobey glanced toward the walking path. "Looks like your aunt and sister are on their way back. Are you sure Aunt Ellen will be okay on her own this weekend?"

"She'll be fine. I'll have our neighbor keep an eye on things, but Aunt Ellen can take care of herself quite well for a few days."

Ellen and Gretchen rejoined them then and Tobey let the subject drop. He and Gretchen got into a lengthy discussion of everything she could expect for the upcoming weekend—plans he had made for her, track rules she would have to follow, the schedule of race events, even an invitation for her to watch the race from the top of the hauler with her own set of headphones to hear the action. She was positively giddy with excitement.

After a while, Aunt Ellen gathered her knitting together and stuffed it in her canvas tote bag. "I guess it's time for us to be getting back home," she said, her subtle signal that she was growing tired.

"I'm not ready to go yet." Gretchen hopped to her feet, a familiar stubborn look appearing in her eyes. "C'mon, Tobey, let's play some more Frisbee."

Hoping there wouldn't be a scene, Amy leveled a look at her sister. "Get your stuff together, Gretchen. It's time to go."

It was obvious that Gretchen wanted very badly to

rebel. Amy suspected that she didn't like being told what to do in front of Tobey, but wasn't sure how to assert her independence without coming across in a negative light to him.

"Just one more game?" she asked, trying for a whee-dling tone rather than a defiant one. "We never get to do anything together as family on the weekends," she added, inserting a little guilt trip into the mix for Amy.

Gretchen gave Tobey a look that all but begged him to take her side against the spoilsports. Amy was almost amused that he immediately seemed to need to concentrate on retying his sneaker. He was making it quite clear that he wouldn't be drawn into this particular discussion.

"We can stay for just a little while longer," Aunt Ellen conceded. "Fifteen minutes?" she asked, glancing at Amy.

Deciding that was a fair compromise, Amy nodded. She had no clue whether she and her great-aunt were just being fair, or if they were rewarding Gretchen's rebelliousness, but fifteen minutes didn't seem like too much to concede. This parenting job would be difficult even if she really were one, but it became even trickier considering that she was making rules for her teenage sister, not a small child.

Gretchen beamed in response to the small victory. "Thanks. So, Tobey, you want to throw the disk around again?"

He looked up from his securely tied shoe. "Sure, I—"

Before he could finish the sentence, the cell phone clipped to his belt buzzed. He glanced at the screen, then gave Gretchen an apologetic smile. "Excuse me a minute." Lifting the phone to his ear, he said, "Hey, Joey, what's up?"

Even without blatantly eavesdropping on his end of the conversation, it was pretty obvious that there would be no more Frisbee-playing on his part that afternoon. "I'm sorry," he said when he completed the brief call. "I've got to leave now. They need me at the shop."

"On your free Sunday?" Aunt Ellen clucked and shook her head. "Don't they let you have even one day off?"

"That's the nature of the job," he said with a light shrug. "Now you know why I stay single."

He'd obviously meant it as a joke, but the comment fell rather flat. Looking a little flustered, he thanked them again for inviting him, told Gretchen he would see her in a few days and rushed away, leaving all three women gazing after him.

Making herself move, Amy stood and shook out the quilt before folding it. "Gretchen, will you throw that trash into the container, please? And then you can carry Aunt Ellen's chair to the car."

This time Gretchen chose to cooperate. "I wish Tobey didn't have to leave," she said as she tossed paper napkins into a nearby receptacle. "He could have come to our house and played video games or something."

"I'm sure Tobey has plenty of other things to do," Amy replied. "He's a very busy man. I was surprised he could join us for the picnic."

Gretchen folded the canvas chair. "He made time because he likes being with us."

"Well, yes," Amy acknowledged, stowing the picnic things in the back of her car. "But don't get too used to having him around, Gretchen. It's just been coincidence that he was free this afternoon. Just a transition period while he and I got used to working together."

"Kent didn't hang out with us when you were getting used to working with him," Gretchen countered, fastening her safety belt in the seat behind Amy's.

Amy didn't really have an answer for that. She just hoped Gretchen wasn't reading too much into Tobey's temporary presence in their lives.

She was having to give herself that very same warning every so often.

CHAPTER TEN

"WHAT THE HELL is this?"

Startled, Amy jumped and looked up from her computer screen in her office as a thin stack of papers landed on the desk beside her. "Tobey, you scared me half to death."

He looked more annoyed than repentant, though he muttered a perfunctory, "Sorry. But what is that?"

She glanced at the paper, recognized the subject and looked back up at him. "It's an ad campaign for Easy Jeans. You know, Kent's second biggest sponsor?"

"I know who Kent's sponsors are," he all but snapped back. "What I don't know is what makes you think I'd pose for a bunch of pictures like some sort of male model. Kent's the product in this operation, not me."

"It wouldn't be just you in the ads," she pointed out in a soothing tone. "It's you and Kent and some pretty models posing as admiring fans. You know, the Maximus Motorsports racing team looking good in Easy Jeans. I thought the idea was sort of cute when Debbie from the ad agency suggested it."

"Cute?" His eyes narrowed. "You thought me and

Kent strutting around with a camera aimed at our butts would be 'cute'?"

She resisted an impulse to roll her eyes. "The camera wouldn't be aimed at your… It's a jeans ad, Tobey."

"So have Kent pose for them. He's the one they're sponsoring."

"They're sponsoring the team," she reminded him flatly. "Kent's the driver. You're his new crew chief. You've both been in the spotlight quite a bit lately. You're both young and great-looking and in excellent physical shape, and any guy would want to look so good in their jeans. It makes perfect sense when you look at it that way. The sponsor's going to love it, and the ads could bring new fans to the team. It's not much different than all the interviews and appearances you've already done."

He looked embarrassed, but she didn't know whether it was because of her description of him, or the whole idea. He stabbed a finger at a rough sketch at the bottom of one of the pages. The male figure in the drawing leaned against a race car, apparently wearing nothing but a pair of jeans. "You really think I'd pose bare-chested for an ad campaign? Forget it."

"Actually, I think that's supposed to be me," Kent drawled, entering the office in time to hear the question. "I saw the proposal earlier. Amy sent me copies, too."

Tobey whipped his head around. "And you're okay with this?"

Kent shrugged. "It's just another ad. They pay well, and keep the sponsors happy. Part of the job."

"Part of *your* job. Not mine."

Amy noticed that Kent was beginning to look annoyed. She spoke quickly. "It's really not that big a deal, Tobey. Half a day, maybe. They'll juggle your schedule and Kent's so it won't interfere too badly with your work. And it really does pay well."

The stubborn look on Tobey's face reminded her a bit of Gretchen just then. "I get paid well enough as it is. My job is to help this team win races. That doesn't include strutting around like a peacock to sell jeans."

"Hey." Kent looked genuinely irritated now. "Thanks a lot, Harris. You think I'm not as committed to racing as you are? You think I wouldn't rather be behind a steering wheel than in front of a camera? Everyone knows there's a lot more emphasis on public relations these days than there used to be, but that doesn't make any of us less focused on winning."

Tobey sighed heavily and pushed a hand through his hair. "I didn't mean it that way. I know autographs and advertising and public appearances are all part of being a champion driver. I just didn't think I'd have to get caught up in it myself. I have a hard enough time being taken seriously with this 'baby face,' as Amy called it."

Amy managed not to flinch. Even after the pleasant times they had shared during the past few weeks, apparently that comment still stung. "Listen, Tobey, if you really don't want to do this, you certainly don't have to. I'm sure the Easy Jeans ads can be redesigned to feature Kent alone. That would be fine with you, wouldn't it, Kent?"

Kent nodded. "Yeah, whatever. Just tell me where to be and when. And leave me a little time to drive, all right?"

Still frowning, Kent left the room abruptly, not looking at his crew chief on the way out.

Hissing out a breath, Tobey pushed his hand through his hair again, leaving it an appealing mess. "Now I've made Kent mad. Great."

"You, um, don't seem to be in a very good mood today," Amy commented carefully, struck by the difference in him from the picnic yesterday to this display of temper today. "Is something wrong?"

He didn't meet her eyes. "I've just had a lousy day. I'd better get back down to the shop. I'll talk to you later."

"So you want me to turn down this offer on your behalf?" she asked his back.

"I'll think about it," he said on his way out. "Give me a couple of days."

She looked at the doorway through which he had disappeared, shaking her head in disbelief. She'd seen Kent in bad moods, and most of the other members of the team at one point or another. But she'd never seen Tobey quite like that. Was it something she had done? She didn't see how it could be. They hadn't seen each other since that genial picnic the day before.

"I've got some deliveries for you, Amy," Linda, the receptionist, said, entering the office with a stack of thick envelopes. "They came in before you got here today."

"Thank you," she said, waving a hand to indicate that Linda should stack the packages on the corner of the desk.

"Shame about Danny being let go, huh? I thought he was kind of cute."

"Danny?" Amy visualized a tall, thin, thirty-something engine specialist who'd been with Maximus Motorsports for several years as far as she knew. Certainly longer than she had. "What about him?"

Linda lowered her voice to gossip-level. "Everyone's saying that Tobey fired him this morning. Apparently there was a big scene in the shops."

Amy hadn't heard a thing about it. But she hadn't been there that morning, having attended a meeting at Motor Media Group headquarters with her boss, Sandra Jacobs. "I didn't know."

"Couple of other guys threatened to quit, I heard, but apparently Tobey was able to smooth things over with them. I heard Joey wanted Tobey to ask Kent to step in and help calm everything down, but Tobey insisted on dealing with it all himself."

Realizing that they shouldn't be gossiping, Amy quickly shook her head and turned her gaze back to her computer. "Thanks for bringing me the packages, Linda. Is there anything else?"

"Um, no. I guess not." Linda seemed a bit disappointed that the scandal-fest was over, but she left the office without trying to stall any longer.

So that was why Tobey had been in such a foul mood, Amy mused. He must have hated having to let Danny go.

Tobey had always been the one to stand up for anyone who got caught up in Neil's temper tantrums. Neil had had a habit of impulsively firing anyone who annoyed him—Tobey, included, once or twice—but Tobey and Kent had usually been able to get them rehired when they deserved to be. Danny and Tobey must really have had a serious falling out if Tobey had felt the situation called for such drastic action. But he still would have hated having to do it.

She wondered who else had given him problems since he'd taken over Neil's job. And she wondered if Kent agreed with Tobey's decision concerning Danny. Could a difference of opinion there have been partially behind the flare-up between Tobey and Kent in her office?

She tried to concentrate on work for the next few hours, but it wasn't easy. She couldn't help worrying about Tobey. She told herself he could handle the job, and that there were always problems to deal with in a high-pressure position like his. But she still fretted for him.

And she couldn't help wondering why he hadn't told her about what had happened.

Stuffing some paperwork into her tote bag to take home with her, she left her office just before six. She found herself pausing in front of Tobey's closed office door. She wasn't sure if he was in there, since he didn't spend much time at his desk, but she thought she heard muted sounds through the door. Tentatively, she tapped on the wood.

"Come in," he called out.

Swallowing, she opened the door.

Tobey sat at his desk, his computer open in front of him, stacks of papers scattered around him. His blond-and-brown hair was even messier than before, if possible, which meant he'd had his hands in it again. He glanced up when she stepped in. He smiled perfunctorily, but it didn't lighten his shadowed eyes. "Amy. What can I do for you?"

"Nothing. I'm just on my way out and I wanted to see if you're okay."

He glanced at his computer screen, probably as a way to keep from meeting her eyes. "I'm fine. Thanks for asking."

"I heard what happened this morning. That couldn't have been easy for you."

"No. It wasn't."

"Do you want to talk about it?"

He hesitated for a moment, then shook his head. "Not just now. But thank you."

"Okay. I guess I'll go, then."

"All right. I'll see you tomorrow."

She turned and moved toward the hallway. Tobey said her name, which made her pause and turn back. "Yes?"

"Thank you," he said again, and this time he seemed to mean it.

She nodded. "Call if you change your mind about wanting to talk. Good night, Tobey."

"G'night, Amy."

She closed the door behind her, reluctantly leaving him alone with his grim thoughts.

IT WAS AFTER nine by the time Tobey walked into his apartment that evening. He glanced around the living room, noting that the cleaning lady had been in that day.

Every surface gleamed and the air smelled of lemon cleaners and floral air fresheners. He was here so rarely that dust and mustiness were her main purposes in coming twice a month.

Moving into the kitchen, he opened the fridge and glumly studied its sparse contents. Not much there in the way of food. He pulled out a canned drink and looked in the equally barren pantry for something that might be considered dinner. A can of chicken noodle soup caught his eye. He heated it in the microwave and sat at the breakfast bar to eat it with a few stale crackers. He didn't bother turning on the TV for noise.

For some reason, he found himself thinking about the meals he had eaten with Amy's family. The feminine chatter and clatter of cutlery, the tantalizing aromas of home-cooked food. The memories made this solitary bowl of soup seem even more pathetic.

He washed his bowl and spoon and put them away, then carried his drink into the living room. His gaze fell immediately on the telephone he'd left sitting on the table with his car keys, and he felt the urge to pick it up and dial Amy's number. He resisted, telling himself it was too late to call her. He didn't know what he would have said, anyway.

He'd been really snarly to her earlier. She hadn't deserved that. He truly had hated the idea of the advertising photos, but he could have told her so without the surliness that he had also turned toward Kent. Not a wise move, either way.

Jenny used to needle him about his temper, he

remembered, as he slumped into an easy chair. She'd said it took an awful lot to set it off, but once ignited, it had scorched everyone in his vicinity. He was usually the peacemaker, the mediator. Yet when he was in one of his rare bad moods, he was known to snap at bystanders for the flimsiest of excuses. He'd snarled at Jenny that way a few times, he remembered with a familiar, heavy guilt.

This wasn't the time to think about Jenny, he told himself flatly, sitting up straighter in the chair. After the day he'd had, futile self-recriminations would only lead to a depression he wasn't sure he could climb out of by morning.

Somehow the phone was in his hand without him even being aware of reaching for it. He looked down at it, torn by indecision. And then he opened it, telling himself that Amy would have turned off her own phone if it was too late for calls.

She answered on the second ring. He figured she'd seen his number on the screen from the way she said, "Hello."

"Hi. Is this a bad time?"

"No. I was just looking over some paperwork before turning in. Aunt Ellen's already in bed and Gretchen's watching the end of a DVD she rented for tonight, so it's pretty quiet here tonight."

It sounded nice to him. Warm. Homey. He looked around his empty room and told himself he liked not having to worry about what anyone else was doing just then.

"The reason I called," he said after taking a deep

breath to brace himself, "was to apologize for the way I talked to you earlier. I shouldn't have snapped at you, and I'm sorry."

"I understand. You'd had a bad morning and the ad campaign proposal caught you off guard."

She was letting him off entirely too easily. "Still, all you did was pass along the offer. You didn't deserve to be yelled at."

"Okay," she said with a quiet laugh, "I accept your apology. You can stop now."

"Fine." He knew when to let something go. "Thanks."

"Really bad day, huh?"

"Lousy," he replied flatly. "The worst I've had as crew chief."

"I'm sorry, Tobey."

"Yeah, me, too. I hated having to let Danny go, Amy. I've been trying to avoid it for the past three weeks. But he just couldn't accept me in Neil's place."

"I don't get that. Surely he saw what a mess Neil had become."

"All he saw was a longtime friend who had gotten pretty lax in the rules. Danny had gotten used to doing his own thing the past few months, and some problems were cropping up because of it. When I tried to make changes, he fought me. I gave him an ultimatum, and he called my bluff. I had no choice but to fire him."

"I'm sure you didn't."

"I'm not like Neil," he said, wincing at the defensiveness he heard in his own voice. "I don't fire people on a whim. And once I've made a decision, I won't go back on it. I'm not going to hire Danny back. Not after the things he said in front of everyone."

"Of course not. That would undermine your authority. You have to make it clear that you're in charge."

He was glad she understood. "Yeah. It's not like I'm trying to be a dictator. I told everyone that I'm open to suggestions and criticism—as long as it's done in a constructive manner."

"I can't imagine anyone thinking of you as a dictator. And I can't understand why Danny was so hostile toward you."

"From the things he said, I think Neil convinced him that I schemed against Neil. Got him fired so I could take his place."

"That's ridiculous. Everyone on the team with even minimal powers of observation should know better than that. Even I saw what was going on, and I didn't know Neil as long as the rest of you did."

Her fierce defense of him was making him feel better about the events of the day. He realized now that he'd called her for that very reason. Somehow he had known that talking to her would help.

"I just hope we can get past this quickly," he confessed. "We can't win races if we can't perform as a team—all of us, from the shop to the pits."

"I know. You'll work it out, Tobey."

"I hope so." He hesitated, then said quietly, "I really put both feet in my mouth with Kent. I've been told I don't always think before speaking when I'm in a bad mood, and I guess I proved that again today."

"Don't worry about it. He'll get over it. I've heard Kent snarl a few times, too, when things aren't going so well for him. Heck, I've done so myself. Just ask Gretchen."

She made it sound like no big deal. Jenny would have made him grovel, he thought with a swallow. She'd have played his guilt for all it was worth.

But he definitely did not want to think about Jenny now. He wasn't quite that masochistic.

"It's getting late," he said, catching a glimpse of the clock on the wall. "I'd better let you get some rest. How about letting me buy you lunch tomorrow?"

"I'm sorry, I can't tomorrow. I have a lunch meeting already scheduled." She sounded genuinely regretful, but he didn't know if she was only being polite.

One way to find out. "Then how about dinner instead? Just the two of us, for a change."

"Okay. Sure, that would be nice."

"Great. So, I'll see you tomorrow, then."

"Yes. Good night, Tobey."

"G'night, Amy."

He disconnected the call feeling much better than he had before he'd talked to her. He'd gone from being disgruntled about everything to having something to look forward to the next evening.

It must have been indicative of his convoluted mood that even that thought made him a little uneasy.

"SERIOUSLY?" Gretchen demanded when Amy walked out of her bedroom the next evening. "This is what you're wearing on a date?"

Because Amy knew her fitted, V-necked brown top and loose tan slacks were perfectly appropriate for the evening ahead, she answered mildly, "It isn't a date. Exactly."

"Yeah? Then what is it? Exactly?"

"I'm just having dinner with Tobey." Even she knew how lame that sounded, she thought with a wince.

"Mmm," Gretchen muttered. "And the two of you just happen to have been spending a lot of time together lately. And just happen to be single and unattached and totally cute together."

Sitting in her chair with her knitting, Aunt Ellen made a sound that very much resembled a swallowed laugh. Amy threw a look her way, then moved toward the door. "I hear a car in the driveway. That will be Tobey. I'll just meet him outside to avoid any potential embarrassment from you two."

"But I want to say hi to him," Gretchen protested. "I won't embarrass you, I promise."

Amy already had her hand on the doorknob. "You'll see plenty of him this weekend. Good night, you two."

"Take your time coming home," Aunt Ellen called out. "Gretchen and I will be just fine."

Shaking her head, Amy stepped outside to meet Tobey.

Four hours later, she and Tobey climbed back into his low-slung sports car in the parking lot of a theater where they had just seen a movie together. It had been a spur-of-the-moment thing, resulting from a random comment she'd made during their dinner conversation. They'd been talking about how she hadn't had time to go see a movie in months, and that there was one in particular playing now that she planned to see when she got the chance, and the next thing she knew, they were sitting side by side in a darkened theater with a tub of popcorn to share between them.

She knew the movie had been as unplanned for him as it had been for her. He'd probably intended to return to the shop, just as she'd predicted he would before he'd picked her up. But one thing had led to another and…maybe they had both just wanted a reason to prolong their time together.

"I really enjoyed that," Tobey said as they closed themselves into his car. "Like I said earlier, it's been months since I made time to see a movie in a theater, and the last one I saw was a waste of two hours I could have been working. This one, though, was really good."

"I enjoyed it, too."

He slanted a smile her way. "I'm glad."

Turning sideways in the seat, she studied him, noting that he looked completely relaxed now. "You seem to be in a better mood today than yesterday."

He nodded. They'd already talked about how things had settled down at the shop, and that he'd had a couple of productive meetings with team members that morning. She thought he'd seemed more optimistic about winning over the few who still doubted that he was the right guy to replace Neil, and to do so without having to let anyone else go. She knew how important that was to him.

"I credit you with my improved mood," he murmured,

reaching across to brush his thumb against her cheek. "I really appreciated the pep talk last night."

He left a little trail of heat when his thumb made a lazy rotation against her skin. It took a bit of effort for her to reply coherently. "I'm always happy to help."

He leaned closer to her, his gaze holding hers. "Amy?"

He'd parked at the back of the lot, so there weren't a lot of people moving around outside the car. Still she'd been aware of some movement and muted voices…until that moment. Until everything outside the vehicle seemed to fade into obscurity. Until all she could see was his face in the shadowy interior, and all she could hear was the sound of her own heartbeat echoing in her ears.

He'd said her name, and he'd made it a question. She blinked and murmured, "Mmm?"

He leaned closer, obviously intending to kiss her, then was stopped by the shoulder strap of the seat belt he'd fastened when he climbed into the car. Impatiently, he released the buckle and reached for her again.

She went into his arms without hesitation.

Each time they kissed, the emotions between them ramped higher, she thought dazedly, her right hand spearing into the back of his soft, tousled hair. Every time he held her, it felt more right to be with him. And every time the kisses ended, she was left wanting more.

His expression when he drew a couple of inches away told her he felt much the same way, at least about the latter sentiment.

Cupping her face between his hands, he asked in a

low growl, "Do you know what I thought the first time I saw you?"

She answered in a whisper. "No. What?"

"I thought you had the most kissable mouth I'd ever seen. And because I knew that sounded sort of sexist when I'd just been introduced to you in a professional context, I made a special effort to notice how good you were at your job and how valuable you were to Kent and to the rest of the team. But I just couldn't help looking at your mouth sometimes and wondering what it would be like to kiss you. Does that annoy you?"

She laughed shakily. "Do you know what I thought the first time I saw you?"

He grimaced. "That I looked too young to be out of high school?"

"No. I thought you looked young, of course—but I also thought you were great-looking. And I wanted to run my hands through your hair." She indulged herself by doing so now. He really did have amazingly thick, soft hair. Incredible blue eyes. The sexiest mouth of any man she knew. Not to mention a body that just begged her hands to explore further...

He kissed her again, a long, slow, deep kiss that made her heart clench and then trip over itself. She couldn't remember ever responding this intensely to only a kiss. Couldn't remember ever feeling quite this same way about anyone before. And wasn't it ironic that she had waited this long to fall this hard? This recklessly?

He lifted his head eventually, giving them both a chance to draw in shaky breaths. Dragging his gaze away from hers, he glanced around, giving a short laugh. "This isn't exactly the place for this, I guess."

A few people walked past outside and the sounds of talking and laughter and passing traffic began to filter into her consciousness. She gave him a weak smile and pushed her hair away from her face. "It's really not."

"So…you want me to take you home now?" He watched her face as he asked the question, and they both knew he was giving her another choice. One she wasn't quite ready to accept.

"Yes," she said with some reluctance, "I suppose you'd better. It's getting late."

He nodded and turned to reach for his seat belt again.

Amy moistened her lips as the car's engine purred to life. "Tobey, you have to admit, this is a little…awkward."

He glanced in the rearview mirror and backed out of the parking space. "In what way?" he asked without inflection.

"In several ways. We're both very busy with our jobs right now."

"True," he acknowledged, driving out of the parking lot. "But we've managed to find a couple hours here and there to spend together during the past few weeks. Tonight, for example."

"Well, yes, but…the fact that we work together makes it a little stickier. I mean, what if you and I have a falling out or something? We still have to work together nearly every day. Despite my attraction to you, I can't risk losing my job, or causing unnecessary complications that give anyone reason to doubt my professionalism."

"We're both mature adults. We can keep our personal issues out of our jobs."

"Neil couldn't," she murmured.

She watched Tobey swallow, and she knew her point had been made. She could see that, despite his casual tone, he shared some of her concerns.

He cleared his throat. "Okay, I know it's a little risky. Sure, I've had some of the same reservations. Frankly, that's why I waited as long as I did to ask you out. Some people have a hard time understanding that my job comes first for me. I've worked damned hard to make crew chief, and I'm going to give everything I've got to being successful at it. I work long hours and I don't have a whole lot left over to offer anyone. All I'm really looking for at this point is someone to talk to, to have fun with, to relax with for a couple of hours, but who still understands that I'm on call pretty much 24/7 if I'm needed.

"We're a lot alike, you and I," he added. "You've just been promoted to your position, too, after working hard to get here, and as you just said, you don't want to do anything to mess it up. But the thing is, regardless of the complications, I still want to see you, Amy. I enjoy being with you. I even like hanging out with your family. And you should know by now that I'm very attracted to you. We can have fun together in our rare off-hours without letting things get out of hand, can't we?"

So, he'd made his position quite clear. He wasn't looking for anything serious or lasting. He saw them as good friends—maybe, if things developed that direction, "friends with benefits." An easy affair, casual,

176   RISKY MOVES

amusing, with a little risk added for spice. But temporary. When one or both tired of the personal relationship, he imagined them genially moving on, their work situation unchanged, their hearts unbruised.

A little naive, maybe, but then, she wasn't looking for anything serious, either, she mused, trying to quell an unexpected sense of disappointment. She tried to comfort herself with the reminder that she certainly didn't have any spare time for anything more than an occasional dinner or movie. Her job was just taking off, Gretchen was just entering the most precarious teenage years and Aunt Ellen was facing the inevitable difficulties of aging, leaving much of the responsibility on Amy's shoulders.

But even though it wouldn't lead to a lifetime commitment, should that mean that she couldn't enjoy spending time with a man whose life was as busy and challenging as her own? Especially since he was the first man in a long time who reminded her that she was a young, healthy woman who'd neglected her own needs for far too long?

"I like being with you, too," she said, settling more comfortably into her seat. "But let's just take it kind of slowly, okay? Just to make sure we're not making a mistake."

He gave a little shrug. "I don't have a problem with that. I'm going to be pretty busy for the rest of this week, anyway. Got to make up for the time I took off tonight."

She thought of the e-mails that would be waiting for her when she got home. "I know the feeling."

"Figured you would. But maybe we can grab a quick lunch together when we're both free?"

She smiled. "I think that can be arranged."

He nodded in satisfaction.

"There's no need to walk me to the door," she said when he parked in her driveway. "Gretchen's liable to try to ambush you and drag you inside."

He chuckled. "I wouldn't mind seeing her and your aunt, but I've got a couple more things I need to attend to tonight."

"So do I. So we'll say good-night here."

He reached out to snag a hand at the back of her head. "Something to tide me over until the next time we can find a few minutes to spend together," he murmured.

Smiling, she closed the distance between them and gave him a kiss calculated to leave him counting the minutes until that next time.

She knew she would be, she thought as she watched him drive away, her lips still tingling and her heart still pounding from that good-night kiss.

CHAPTER ELEVEN

"I FREAKING LOVE being in California!"

Amy heaved a long-suffering sigh. "Settle down, Gretchen, okay?"

She had probably said that a dozen or more times since she and Gretchen departed on their big trip. Gretchen had practically bounced off the walls that morning, too excited to eat breakfast, having to be reminded to pack her toothbrush and to kiss her great-aunt goodbye. She'd fussed over her hair and clothing until Amy had warned her they would be late, and had begged to be allowed to wear makeup for the trip.

Amy usually approved only a little lip gloss for Gretchen's everyday makeup wear, but on special occasions she allowed a little light-toned eye shadow and brown mascara. She deemed today a special occasion, to Gretchen's delight. That, of course, required another fifteen minutes of primping.

Kent and Tanya had been warmly welcoming when Amy and Gretchen joined them on Kent's plane. Tobey showed up, as well, having been invited to be a part of the travel party. Not only would this be Gretchen's first race, but it was also her first time on a airplane, and Kent made sure it was a special event for her, taking her on a tour, serving her snacks, treating her like a VIP guest. Amy was impressed—as was Gretchen, of course.

Tanya talked to Gretchen when Amy, Kent and Tobey fell in to a detailed business discussion. Amy had warned her sister from the outset that she was not to interfere with Amy's responsibilities that weekend, and that there would be many of them. Amy still secretly worried about how she would be able to perform her job and monitor her sister, but she told herself that it wasn't as if Gretchen was a small child. Fourteen was an age that came with its own challenges, but at least she was old enough to follow instructions. For the most part.

Gretchen had a wonderful time both Friday and Saturday. She toured the track, met many NASCAR notables, went on area field trips with other teenagers through the family outreach program and made so many new friends that Amy wondered how Gretchen remembered all their names. She was on her best behavior, giving her older sister no resistance when Amy set down rules for the weekend. Nor did she interfere with Amy's work, calling only a couple of times from her own cell phone to seek permission or give updates on her activities.

Tobey had been smugly satisfied that the weekend was going so well. He'd spent his free time with Amy and Gretchen, seeming not to mind at all that the girl was the center of attention when they were together. Which, of course, only made Amy fall harder for him.

"I can't help it." Gretchen did a quick spin on her

sneakers, her hands clapped in front of her, her flouncy yellow summer shirt swirling around her like a dance of sunbeams. "I'm just happy."

Softening, Amy reached out to smooth her sister's tousled brown hair. "I'm glad you're having a good time."

"The field trip today was so much fun. I took, like, a million pictures on my cell at the movie studio. I can't wait to show them to you."

"I'll look at them as soon as I have time," Amy promised. "Maybe we can do that tonight when we get back to the hotel."

Gretchen nodded eagerly. "So what are we going to do now?"

"We're having dinner tonight with Tobey, Kent and Tanya, and Mr. and Mrs. Ritter. We'll be going to a very nice restaurant, so you'll need to be on your best behavior and use your best table manners."

Gretchen huffed in indignation. "Thanks a lot, Amy."

Amy grimaced apologetically. "I'm sorry. I didn't mean to treat you like a kid. I know that irritates you."

Gretchen nodded, satisfied that she'd made her point. "So, when are we going to go change? I'm wearing that new dress we got last week, right?"

"Right. Tobey's picking us up in an hour to take us to the restaurant, so we'll have to hurry."

"I can't wait to tell Tobey all about my day," Gretchen said, falling into step beside her. "I know he'll want to hear everything."

Amy kept her opinion about that to herself, mentally apologizing to Tobey for the earful he'd be getting that evening. Of course, to his credit, he would give Gretchen his complete attention, with every indication that he was fascinated by everything she said. Amy would cut in to rescue him occasionally, offering him a chance to talk to someone else.

She realized later that she needn't have worried about Gretchen's manners for dinner. Aunt Ellen had done an excellent job of drilling etiquette lessons into the girl.

Looking absolutely lovely in the brown-and-coral-print halter dress she and Amy had selected for that evening, Gretchen behaved as though having dinner in elegant restaurants was something she did all the time. Amy saw the slight indications of nerves, but only because she knew her younger sister so well.

Everyone was in a good mood that evening. Kent had qualified well, and would be starting in fourth position, the outside second row. He had few complaints about the handling of his car, and seemed optimistic that he could finish at or near the top.

The Ritters had selected an old, but elegant, dinner-and-dancing restaurant in which to entertain their guests. White-linened dining tables surrounded a glossy wooden dance floor two steps down from the dining level. An orchestra played ballroom dance music at a volume that still allowed conversation at the candlelit tables. Gretchen was visibly delighted by the comfortable sophistication of the place, her eager brown eyes darting from the laughing, well-dressed diners around them to the dance floor that had not yet opened for dancing.

The Ritters were charmed by her, and both catered

to her shamelessly, suggesting foods she might like, urging her to try bites of theirs, ordering special desserts for her. Kent and Tobey flirted lightly with her, making her blush and giggle, and Tanya asked questions about the activities in which Gretchen had participated. Gretchen was the center of attention during the meal, and she loved every minute of it.

With a little ripple of old, too-familiar pain, Amy thought of how proud her parents would be to see their baby girl now.

"Amy?" Tobey had leaned closer to her, speaking in a low voice that only she could hear since everyone else was involved in a conversation about Gretchen's field trip that morning. "You okay?"

She glanced at him with a smile. "Yes, I'm fine, thank you."

"You're sure? Because you looked a little sad."

She shook her head, a bit startled that he'd read her fleeting emotions so well. "It's nothing, Tobey. But thanks."

Looking only partially satisfied, he nodded and sat back in his seat.

The orchestra began to play a new set and Gretchen craned around in her seat to watch as a few couples took to the dance floor.

"Dawson, they're playing 'Stardust.'" Anna stood, making candlelight glitter in the diamonds she wore at ears, throat, wrists and fingers. The sequined gold top she wore with silky, wide-leg black pants sparkled when she reached determinedly for her husband's hand. "We always dance to 'Stardust,'" she said over her shoulder as she towed him toward the dance floor.

Gretchen giggled. "I like her."

"Everyone likes Anna," Tobey assured her.

"Erica didn't," Tanya muttered, making everyone's smile fade.

"Who's Erica?" Gretchen wanted to know, looking around in surprise at all the suddenly grim faces.

Erica had been Neil's on-again, off-again girlfriend, and a big part of the reason he'd lost his job, in Amy's opinion. She couldn't stand the other woman, and knew that her dining companions felt the same way. "Just someone we used to know," she said to her sister, and then changed the subject. "Do you want some more iced tea?"

Gretchen shook her head, still looking at the dance floor. "Mr. and Mrs. Ritter dance great together, don't they?"

Kent pushed himself to his feet. Amy assumed he was going to ask Tanya to dance, but he surprised her by turning to Gretchen instead. "May I have this dance, Miss Barber?"

Wide-eyed, Gretchen looked first at Tanya, who smiled and nodded, and then at Amy, who shrugged lightly. "Go ahead," she encouraged. "Aunt Ellen didn't insist you take the junior ballroom class earlier this summer for nothing."

Those lessons, along with riding lessons and a church-sponsored Wednesday-night program for teens, had been a way of keeping Gretchen busy during the time off school.

Her cheeks very pink, Gretchen placed her hand on Kent's arm and allowed him to lead her to the dance floor.

"That," Tanya said dreamily, watching the couple ease into a simple box step, "is about the sweetest thing I've ever seen."

Tobey gave Amy a wry look just short of rolling his eyes. "Oh, yeah. Sweet," he muttered.

Tanya had the grace to laugh at herself. "Okay, I know I'm being all sappy. But Kent's really good with kids, isn't he?"

"He is," Amy agreed. "I've told him so several times after he's met with children for various events."

Her eyes going somber, Tanya continued to watch her fiancé. "It's nice to see him smile like that again. With everything going on in his family, he's been so distracted lately. He's obviously having a great time tonight, and he needed that."

Amy and Tobey shared another glance. Neither of them would be comfortable gossiping about Kent's family troubles, but everyone in the sport knew about the tension in the Grosso clan. It couldn't be easy for Kent to concentrate on work when his family was in turmoil. But he had generously made sure that Gretchen had a wonderful weekend, and Amy would always be grateful to him for that.

It wasn't much later when Tobey drove the sisters back to their hotel, after one dance each with both Amy and Gretchen. "Did you have a good time, Gretchen?" he asked as he gallantly escorted them to their door.

"I had the best time ever," she answered with a happy sigh.

Amy thought Gretchen was beginning to look a bit tired, though she knew she wouldn't admit it. It had been a long, busy day.

Amy swiped the key card to unlock the door of their room. Gretchen hesitated before going in, then threw her arms around Tobey's waist. "Thank you for taking us to dinner," she said warmly.

He looked a little startled, but returned the hug. "You're welcome. But Mr. Ritter picked up the check for dinner," he added candidly.

Gretchen smiled as she drew back. "I'll send him a thank-you note when I get home," she promised. "But you're still the one who put this trip together for me, and I just want you to know how great it's been."

"I'm glad you're enjoying it." Tobey reached out to catch Amy's wrist, a signal that he wanted to speak with her alone.

Amy motioned toward the door. "Go on in, Gretchen, I'll be there in a minute."

"Okay. G'night, Tobey."

"Good night, Gretchen. See you tomorrow."

Gretchen closed the door behind her when she went inside the room.

Glancing up at Tobey, Amy waited for him to speak first. Reading her expression, he smiled. "I didn't really have anything to say. I just wanted a couple minutes alone with you."

She glanced down the hallway, which—for the

moment—was unoccupied except for the two of them. "You'd better make it fast."

"I can do that." Before he'd finished speaking, he had her in his arms, her smile crushed beneath his own.

KENT AND TOBEY were scheduled for an early sponsor breakfast meet-and-greet Sunday morning. Vittle Farms had put on a spread for local business associates and dignitaries, and Kent made a short speech while they ate, thanking everyone for their support of the Maximus Motorsports Vittle Farms team. Tobey also made a brief talk, assuring everyone that another championship for the Vittle Farms team was top priority for him. Afterward, they sat side by side at a table and signed autographs.

There'd been no need for Amy to join them that morning, so she had taken Gretchen to the nondenominational church service for racing families. Tobey attended the services himself, when his schedule allowed, which, he admitted, hadn't happened since his promotion.

He glanced at his watch as he and Kent made their escape from the Vittle Farms suite. They still had a couple of quick promotional stops to make before the drivers' meeting. Kent had a few other appearances scheduled that, mercifully, Tobey didn't have to attend, since he had other responsibilities as the race approached.

Moving from one appearance to another, he watched as Kent was repeatedly approached for autographs. Kent had perfected the art of signing while walking, rarely even interrupting his conversation with his companion, though he did offer friendly smiles to his fans. Stopping would have been a grave mistake on a day so tightly scheduled. Mobs of fans hungry for autographs, conversations and photos with their racing heroes could gather in minutes, causing awkward scenes and delays.

They ducked into the hauler for a quick discussion before they went their separate ways. Kent had thought of just a couple more things he wanted to mention to Tobey about the upcoming race. Tobey had spent several hours late last night watching tapes of last week's pit stops—tapes he had watched until he'd memorized every move that had been recorded—and he'd made a couple of notes he shared with Kent. He would huddle with the pit crew for a last-minute briefing while Kent was participating in opening ceremonies.

Looking at his watch again, he said, "You'd better be going. Amy will have both of our heads if you're late to any of your scheduled appearances."

Kent chuckled. "Yeah, she would. So, uh, you and Amy—getting kind of chummy, aren't you?"

Tobey had no intention of trying to keep secret the fact that he and Amy were seeing each other outside of their jobs. From what he had observed, secrets had a nasty way of being revealed at the most inconvenient times. "Yeah, we've spent some time together."

"Spent time with her family, too, haven't you?" Kent fingered the bracelet he wore that matched the one on Tobey's right wrist. Both of them wore the good-luck charms today in honor of Gretchen's presence.

"Some. I enjoy them."

"I always suspected you had a thing for Amy. Something about the way you looked at her earlier this season. The way you blushed when she walked into a room."

"I didn't blush," Tobey said with a scowl, refusing to believe that his face felt any warmer at that moment. He was accustomed to being teased by his teammates, just as he'd done his share of ribbing in return. But he had a hard time joking about Amy.

"Hey, I'm just kidding. You and Amy seem to be a great match. And Tanya told me last night that she thinks you're a cute couple," he added with another laugh.

Couple? Tobey swallowed. He hadn't really thought of them as a couple.

"We're just…hanging out," he said lamely, finding no other words to describe their vague relationship.

Kent nodded as if it made sense, anyway. "I'd do the big brotherly thing and warn you about treating her right…but I think Amy is quite capable of taking care of herself."

"Yeah, she is. And if you don't get going for that next appointment, she's going to come looking for you and prove she's capable of kicking your behind."

Laughing, Kent headed for the exit. "I'm going, I'm going. See you, chief."

Chief. Kent had called Neil that on occasion. He probably hadn't even realized he'd used the nickname with Tobey just then, but Tobey was very aware of it. To him, it was almost a badge of acceptance. Maybe he was overreacting to a throwaway remark, but he wanted to believe that Kent was truly starting to trust him to be the right man to lead his team.

At least Kent didn't seem to have a problem with Tobey and Amy seeing each other outside of work. He wouldn't blame Kent for worrying that the relationship could interfere with their jobs, but he assumed Kent knew them both better than to think they would let that happen.

Two ambitious, confirmed workaholics, he mused. That was how everyone surely saw both Amy and him. And they were right, of course. They might enjoy a little dalliance on occasion, but when their relationship ended, as it inevitably would, they would both have their jobs to keep them fulfilled. It was all they both wanted at this point, he assured himself.

Realizing he was fingering the beads on Gretchen's bracelet again, he scowled and reached for his clipboard. It was past time for him to get back to his team.

AMY AND GRETCHEN watched the race from the top of the hauler. The Ritters had extended an invitation for Gretchen to join them in their luxury viewing suite, but Amy had thought Gretchen would prefer being out in the middle of everything—and she'd been right. Gretchen loved being up that high, having such a great vantage point for seeing the track, the stands packed with spectators in their colorful fan clothing, the concessions stands and souvenir stands and merchandise trucks and media paraphernalia.

Amy noted that Gretchen couldn't help preening a little because she was privileged to watch the race from such an "insider" position. She wore her track pass around her neck with pride, and beamed every time one of the team members passed by and greeted her by name. Her little sister, Amy thought dryly, had taken very quickly to VIP treatment.

Amy had to duck into the hauler lounge a few times during the race for business calls. She gave permission to Gretchen to climb down for snacks, but warned her not to wander off alone. Nor was she to disturb Tobey, under any circumstances. If Gretchen wanted to go look through the midway of merchandise trailers and food vendors, she should take Josh with her, she added. Tobey had given Josh instructions to drop anything else he might be doing if Amy or Gretchen needed him for anything during the race.

Josh genially agreed, seeming not to mind being asked to babysit the PR rep's kid sister during the race. Amy had yet to see good-natured Josh object to any chore he'd been assigned. He was probably going to go far with the team eventually, she thought with a secret smile.

Obviously delighted to have a pleasantly attractive young man at her beck and call, Gretchen promised not to cause any problems. She seemed content to sit in the shade of a portable awning on the hauler, listening to the chatter through the headphones she'd been given and watching the activities around her, both on and off the track.

Amy was amused when she heard Tobey warn through the headphones that everyone should remember no "cussing." He didn't actually mention Gretchen's name, but she figured everyone knew who he was thinking of when he gave the command. They were always aware their transmissions were being overheard by fans and media and NASCAR officials, but sometimes tongues slipped during the heat of competition.

She would have loved for Kent to win again for many reasons, not the least being that Gretchen would have been thrilled to see him in Victory Lane. Unfortunately, he wasn't able to pull off the repeat. He finished third, which was enough to secure his place in the Chase for the NASCAR Sprint Cup, even if Richmond turned into a catastrophe. She looked around for some wood to knock in hopes that she hadn't jinxed them next week with the thought. She settled for a wood-grained countertop in the hauler.

With typical efficiency, the pit was cleaned out and the hauler packed up almost before Kent finished his postrace interviews. And then a limo whisked them to the airport for the return trip home. Amy saw Gretchen cast one lingering, rather regretful look back toward the track as they drove away. She'd had such a good time that she apparently wasn't quite ready to leave, even though she couldn't wait to give her great-aunt and her friends a moment-by-moment account of her trip.

Back in Charlotte, Gretchen hugged Kent and Tanya, charmingly thanking them both for their kindness. Both invited her to join them again sometime, and it was obvious that they meant it.

"Someday," Amy answered when Gretchen gave her a hopeful look.

As much as she had enjoyed having her sister with her for that one weekend, it wasn't something she

intended to make a habit of. It was just too hard for her
to concentrate on her work with so many distractions.
And her sister, she thought with a glance at Tobey, was
only one of those distractions.

CHAPTER TWELVE

AMY WANTED TO believe that she wasn't the one who jinxed Kent at Richmond. After all, the event wasn't exactly a catastrophe, she told herself afterward. He managed to finish eleventh after a very difficult race fraught with caution flags, tire issues, one almost-botched pit stop and other problems. And he was still in the Chase for the NASCAR Sprint Cup. He finished the race fourth in the point standings.

Though the team congratulated each other on pulling out a decent finish, she could tell that no one was really happy about not ending up in the top ten, especially after the last four races had all concluded so well for Kent. Tobey, she was pleased to see, looked disappointed but resigned. This, too, was part of the job, and he'd proven that he could handle difficulties as well as victories.

Amy and Tobey and Kent were almost inseparable at Richmond. She had her usual responsibilities assisting Kent, of course. Kent and Tobey spent a lot of time huddled together with various other members of the team, trying to overcome the car problems they had all weekend, so she saw a lot of Tobey on the job. With all the obstacles they faced that weekend, Tobey had very little free time—but what he had, he spent with her. Meals, quick coffee breaks, one heart-poundingly steamy interlude in his motor home that ended all too soon when he was summoned back to the garage.

They didn't try to hide their developing relationship, but they didn't overtly call attention to it, either. They kept their kisses in private.

Though the next week was hectic for both of them, they carved out a couple of hours to be together Tuesday evening. They went out for dinner, Chinese this time. Because of Gretchen's allergy to ginger, Amy didn't have Chinese food often. Tobey went through his usual routine of notifying the server of his shellfish allergy, and then they split plates of pot stickers and cashew chicken. They washed it down with cups of oolong tea, and shared a selection of fresh fruits for dessert.

During the meal, they talked about work. About Gretchen, and her mixture of eagerness and anxiety about the first few weeks of school. About favorite books and favorite music and favorite films. Only after she was at home getting ready for bed did it occur to Amy that, once again, she had revealed more of herself than Tobey had.

Odd how she always ended up chattering away about her family, her home life, memories of her past. Tobey, on the other hand, tended to ask questions, react to her stories, encourage her to tell him more without really reciprocating. And he did it so skillfully that she never quite realized what he had done until later.

She knew so little about his past. His family. She sensed that he had a warm, if somewhat distant, relationship with his mother and sisters, and that he liked his stepfather well enough, though he didn't think of him as a father figure. She believed that he'd been close to his biological father and that the loss had been devastating.

During his meals with her family, he had shared a couple of funny stories about things he'd done as a mischievous boy during church services, embarrassing his pastor father and Sunday School-teacher mother. But those anecdotes had been light, amusing, surface-deep, revealing very little that they didn't already know about him. He'd given her very little more when they were alone.

Maybe he just wasn't the type to talk about himself much, she mused, turning the sheets back on her bed. But it was getting increasingly frustrating. They were growing so close in some ways. When they were together, even with other people, they could share a glance and speak volumes.

Kisses—wow. Off the Richter scale. There was no question that the physical chemistry between them was powerful. Even though they had agreed to take this relationship slowly, it wouldn't be long until kisses weren't enough for either of them. But how much was she willing to risk for a man who was still holding back so much of himself?

THERE WAS A NEW attitude at the track in New Hampshire. Amy sensed it not only among her own team, but also among all the other competitors at the track that weekend. And it wasn't only the refreshing promise of fall in the air, or the beauty of the area with the first hints of color appearing in the trees.

The late-in-the-season weariness of the past few weeks had dissipated as the final portion of the Chase began. For the top twelve drivers, each of these last ten races would be a crucial step toward the NASCAR Sprint Cup Series championship. The remaining teams who hadn't made the Chase would compete for purses and final season standings. It would all come to a spectacular end at Miami, with someone—she crossed her fingers that it would be Kent—being crowned champion.

And in February, she thought with a dry smile, everything would be reset and it would all start over again. And after only a couple of months' rest, the teams would be on the road again, single-mindedly focused on racing. On winning. It was a demanding, obsessive, stress-filled life they had all chosen, but she doubted that many had any regrets about getting involved. She knew she couldn't imagine herself being completely happy away from this sport she had grown to love and respect.

As crazy as the weekend was, she and Tobey still found a little time to spend together. They slipped away late Saturday afternoon after practice for coffee and cookies in his motor home.

"Everything is going so well this weekend, I'm half-afraid to even admit it," Tobey said with a crooked smile as he sat across the table from her.

"Kent told me the car is awesome. He seems really encouraged."

"Yeah. Like I said, everything's going well so far."

She knew the past week had been good for Tobey in the shop. He seemed to have most of the personnel problems settled, for now, something he had accomplished by being consistent, firm and fair. He'd always been well liked by the team, and now they were beginning to respect him, too, accepting his authority over them, even though some of them were quite a bit older and had several years of seniority.

When they were finished with their snacks, they carried the dishes to the sink. Amy was rinsing her cup before stacking it in the dishwasher when Tobey's arms went around her from behind.

"It's been hours since we've had a chance to be alone together," he whispered huskily in her ear.

Her knees went weak in response to the warm, hard feel of him against her back. She let herself lean against him, her eyelids going heavy as she savored the feeling. "Yes, it has."

Turning her in his arms, he captured her mouth with his, kissing her until she thought she might just melt into a puddle on the floor. Her arms around his neck were the only thing holding her upright, she thought as his hands began a slow, roving journey over her, leaving sparks of pleasure and desire in their wake.

She crowded closer to him, one hand buried in his luxurious hair, her lips parting to better accommodate his deep, hungry kisses. It wouldn't be much longer until they both had to be back at work, but maybe there was just enough time to…

Her phone rang at her belt, making them both jump and Tobey mutter a curse.

Her hands unsteady, Amy reached for the phone. "It's Gretchen," she said, recognizing the ring tone she'd assigned to her little sister.

Tobey nodded and moved away, drawing deep breaths while she lifted the phone to her ear.

"Aunt Ellen won't let me go to Carson's house," Gretchen complained almost before Amy had said hello. "It's not fair."

Amy sighed heavily, half turning her back to Tobey in the hopes that he wouldn't overhear how trivial the interruption had been. "Gretchen, what have I told you about calling me just to complain? You know you're supposed to do what Aunt Ellen says regardless of whether you agree with her or not."

"But, Amy, we're just going to watch movies and maybe play some video games. And it's not like we'd be the only ones there. His mom works at the hospital on weekends, but his dad's home today."

"I'm sure Aunt Ellen has her reasons for saying no."

"She said it's because Carson's dad is always out in his workshop so me and Carson wouldn't really be supervised—like that matters. And she said that Carson's dad allows him to watch R-rated movies and play violent video games and stuff, but big deal. We're not babies. Besides, I told her I wouldn't watch anything she wouldn't approve of, but it's like she doesn't trust me."

"Why don't you invite Carson over to watch movies at our place instead?"

"That's what Aunt Ellen said. I'd rather go to Carson's. He's got a big-screen TV and all his games are over there. She just wants us here so she can hover over us like we have to be watched every minute or we'll get into trouble or turn into criminals or something."

Amy was well aware that her sister was a young and somewhat overprotected fourteen. Maybe it was time for them to give her a bit more freedom, but Amy wasn't going to undermine Aunt Ellen's authority. Especially not when she wasn't there to deal with the consequences.

"You do what Aunt Ellen says," she repeated. "You can ask Carson over, if you like, and I'm sure she'll try not to embarrass you while he's there."

"But, Amy," Gretchen whined.

"That's it, Gretchen. Take it or leave it. Now, I've got to go. I'll talk to you later."

She disconnected before her sister could start another round of protests.

"Problem?" Tobey asked as she turned slowly back to face him.

She wrapped her arms around her waist. "Gretchen's fighting with Aunt Ellen again."

She couldn't quite read Tobey's expression. Maybe he was finally realizing just how difficult it was to have an easy fling with someone with Amy's responsibilities. But all he said was, "You've mentioned that they don't get along sometimes, but it's hard to imagine the two of them quarreling."

"Oh, it's more than just quarreling. It's outright re-bellion on Gretchen's part. As I've mentioned before, you've only seen her on her best behavior. As long as things are going her way, which they usually are when you're around, she's an angel. But cross her, and she can get pretty difficult."

"What usually causes the arguments?"

"Usually, it's Gretchen wanting to do something Aunt Ellen doesn't approve of. Like having a sleepover without proper parental supervision."

"I would agree with your aunt on that one."

"So did I, actually. Today, Gretchen wanted to go to a boy's house to watch movies and play video games. His father will be there, although outside in his workshop, but Aunt Ellen thought it best if Gretchen invites her friend to our house instead. I think the truth is that she doesn't approve of Gretchen going to a boy's house."

Tobey cocked an eyebrow. "You look as though you don't really agree this time."

"I'm…conflicted," Amy admitted. "I told her to do what Aunt Ellen said, of course, and I didn't express any reservations. But I'm not sure that it would have been so bad if Gretchen spent a couple of hours at Carson's house."

Tobey frowned. "Gretchen's kind of young to be hanging out alone with boys. Doesn't she have any girlfriends?"

She couldn't help smiling a little. He sounded so big brotherly. "Yes, she has girlfriends. But she's fourteen,

Tobey. Maybe Aunt Ellen and I are trying too hard to keep her from growing up."

He started to reply, but was interrupted when her phone rang again. Giving him a glance of apology, she answered it.

"Weren't we supposed to meet at the hauler before that interview?" Kent demanded in her ear.

"I said two-thirty," she answered, glancing at her watch. "It's just five after two now."

"Oh. Sorry, thought you said two."

Kent was pretty hopeless at keeping his schedule straight without her, she thought with a shake of her head. "I'll be there in a few minutes. We'll go over our notes again before the interview."

"I'll be here."

Knowing the mood was effectively ruined, she looked at Tobey as she replaced her phone in its holder. "I guess I should go."

"I'll take you back. The limo awaits," he said with a forced laugh, waving an arm toward the door. "And by limo, of course, I mean golf cart."

Relieved that he'd managed to put his understandable frustration behind him and get into a relatively good mood again, she nodded. "Of course."

"I still think your aunt is right," he said as she reached for her ever-present tote bag. "If Gretchen has to spend time with a boy, it should be at your house where Aunt Ellen can keep an eye on them. It isn't that I wouldn't trust Gretchen," he added, "but that boy could be a problem."

Amy had to laugh a little, though she couldn't help being touched by how protective he was acting about Gretchen. "You sound just like my dad did when I was a teenager and wanted to start dating. If it had been up to him, he'd have gone along as chaperone every time."

Tobey grinned. "I can understand that. If I ever had a daughter, I'd probably…"

His smile suddenly froze, then faded. "Well," he said, opening the outer door, "this is really none of my business. I'm sure you and your aunt know best how to raise your little sister."

She hesitated a moment before stepping outside. "Tobey, is something wrong?"

"No," he assured her without meeting her eyes. "We just have to get back to work."

She nodded and stepped past him outside the motor home. During the brief ride back to the hauler, she couldn't help wondering what, exactly, had been said that had changed Tobey's mood again so radically.

Once again, she realized she didn't have a clue what he was thinking.

KENT FINISHED second at New Hampshire. It was irritating enough to him that he didn't win, but even worse in his opinion that he finished behind Justin Murphy, his longtime rival and his sister's boyfriend. Watching his postrace interviews closely, Amy was pleased to note that he handled the questions well. He skillfully acknowledged all his sponsors, congratulated Justin on his win, firmly evaded personal questions about his family and expressed his confidence that he could still win a second championship. His second place finish had just moved him up to third position in points.

"You did very well, Kent," she assured him when he ducked into the hauler to avoid any further questions. "I'm glad you remembered to mention McGilvey Tools."

"I always remember my sponsors," he said with a shrug.

"I know. But having just signed them on this week, I was afraid you would forget."

"Give me a little credit, Amy."

She held up her hands in a pacifying gesture, knowing he wasn't really annoyed. Just tired. "Sorry. I'm only trying to justify my pay."

Weary and disheveled from the long hours in the car, Kent smiled apologetically and threw am arm casually around her shoulders. "No, I'm sorry," he said with his patented charm. "I didn't mean to snap. You're doing a great job, Amy. You've more than justified your pay."

"Hey. Better not let your fiancée see you with your arm around your PR rep," Tobey said lightly, strolling into the lounge. "She'll have your hide."

"Nah," Kent drawled. "Tanya's not really the jealous type. Are *you*?"

Tobey studied Kent's arm around Amy, and for just a moment an odd gleam appeared in his blue eyes. "I didn't used to think so," he said, and then smiled, his expression smoothed again. "Y'all ready to get out of here so the guys can get the hauler packed up?"

Kent dropped his arm and moved toward the exit. "We're moving, chief."

Tobey stroked a hand down Amy's arm when she moved to follow Kent out. It was just a light, casual gesture, but it had the effect of making her forget any other touch but his.

She wondered if that had been his intention.

TOBEY ASKED Amy out again Tuesday evening, just the two of them.

"Where's he taking you tonight?" Gretchen asked as Amy fastened the back of the silver-and-copper earrings she wore with a black jersey drape-neck top and silvery-gray slacks.

Sliding her feet into a pair of copper-toned heels, she replied, "He said he was going to surprise me."

"Sounds like fun. Must be nice to get to spend time with a guy you like."

"Don't start with me again, Gretchen. There's a big difference between fourteen and thirty-one. Aunt Ellen and I have both told you that you can have Carson over here anytime you want. And we've said it's okay if you go to his house occasionally, as long as at least one of his parents is home. You have to give us your word you won't play mature-rated video games or watch R-rated movies while you're there. We're trusting you to keep your word."

She didn't see the need to add that there would be consequences if they found out that Gretchen wasn't following the rules they had set for her.

Gretchen sighed heavily. "I don't think Carson will ask me over very often if he can't play the games he wants or watch the movies he likes while I'm there."

"Then he isn't much of a friend, is he, if he'd rather do those things than be with you?"

"I'm not a baby, Amy."

"No," she replied with a touch of regret. "You aren't. That's why we've decided you're old enough to be on the honor system in some cases. But you aren't an adult yet, either, and until you are, Aunt Ellen and I have to make rules we think are best for you. Trust me, your rules aren't any stricter than the ones I followed at your age."

"I bet Mom and Dad would've listened to my side," Gretchen muttered.

Amy turned away from the mirror where she'd been making a last-minute check of her appearance. Her heart clenched with grief and guilt, and then started to beat again on a surge of annoyance. "Don't pull that on me, either," she said evenly. "That's just unfair, Gretchen, and you know it."

Gretchen only looked down at the floor and shrugged, her face red with either embarrassment or regret. Maybe a combination of the two.

They both heard the doorbell chime and Gretchen turned and ran out of the room before Amy had a chance to move. She wondered if she should be leaving again tonight when she spent so much time away from her family as it was. Gretchen had certainly managed to ratchet up the guilt factor, she thought wryly.

Gretchen had beaten everyone to the door. "Hi,

Tobey," she said, all sweetness and smiles now. She gave him a hug of greeting. "How's it going?"

Grinning, he tugged at her hair and handed her a small pink gift bag. "It's great. I brought you something from New Hampshire."

"A present for me?" She beamed. "What is it?"

"Open it and see."

Amy hadn't known Tobey was going to bring a gift, so she was almost as curious as her sister when Gretchen dug into the bag. Gretchen pulled out a small box of maple candy, which made her smile in anticipation, and then a square, jewelry-style box. Passing the candy and the gift bag to Amy to hold, she pulled off the top of the box, then gasped in delight.

"Oh, it's so pretty," she exclaimed, lifting out a glittering, clear blue pendant on a fine silver chain. "What is it? Some kind of stone?"

"It's sea glass," he replied. "It's made by a local artist in New Hampshire from pieces of glass that have been tumbled smooth by waves against the beach. One of the other guys bought a couple for his wife and daughter, and I thought you might like one, too. I sent Josh to buy it, because I'm afraid I didn't have time to go pick one out, but I thought he did a good job selecting one."

"It's beautiful. Thank you," Gretchen said, already fastening the trinket around her neck. "And tell Josh he has good taste."

"I will." Looking pleased with her reaction to the

gift, Tobey added, "You gave me a handmade piece of jewelry, so I wanted to return the favor. Unfortunately, I have no artistic skill."

Gretchen laughed and looked in the decorative mirror hanging on the foyer wall. "This is perfect. I can't wait to show it to everyone."

"That *is* pretty," Aunt Ellen approved, having joined them in time to see the opening. "That was nice of you," she added with a nod for Tobey.

"I didn't forget my favorite lady." Tobey handed another small gift bag to Aunt Ellen. "This one's for you."

"Really?" Looking a bit flustered and wholly pleased, Ellen accepted the gift. She pulled out another small box of maple candy, and a scented soy candle in a decorative glass jar. Lifting the lid, she took an appreciative sniff.

"Oh, it smells just like evergreens," she commented. "Like being out in the woods on a crisp fall day. I'll enjoy this, Tobey, thank you. And I'll enjoy the candy, too," she added impishly.

"The candle was also made by a New Hampshire artisan," he commented. "I bought that myself, at a gift shop in a restaurant where Kent and I had a business lunch with Dawson and a sponsor. Kent bought one like it for his great-grandmother, only in a different scent, I think. He said she loves candles."

"As do I." Aunt Ellen reached up to pat his cheek affectionately. "Thank you again, dear. Can I get you anything? A cup of coffee, maybe?"

"No, thanks," he replied, looking a bit embarrassed

by the attention. "Amy and I should be going—if you're ready, Amy?"

"I'm ready." Tucking a clutch purse beneath her arm, she took her leave of her family, then stepped outside with Tobey. "That was nice of you. But you didn't have to bring gifts."

"I wanted to. Like I said, I saw those things in New Hampshire and they made me think of Gretchen and Aunt Ellen."

And yet he hadn't mentioned them to her. She wondered why. "So, where are we going tonight?"

"If it's okay with you, I thought I'd cook tonight."

She half turned in her seat, trying not to sound too surprised when she said, "You're going to cook?"

"Yeah. Don't expect anything too fancy, but even I can throw a couple of steaks on the grill. I put some potatoes in the oven to bake before I left, so they should be done by the time the steaks are finished. And I bought a premixed salad and dessert. Sound okay?"

"Sounds good," she replied, wondering why she suddenly felt so nervous. "I've never even seen your place."

He'd mentioned that he rented an apartment, but he'd never suggested taking her there before. She had to admit that she was curious about his home.

His apartment was in a nice, young-professional-type complex arranged around a central compound with a huge fountain and very nice landscaping. His unit came with a single-car garage. He parked inside it and led her up the stairs into his apartment.

If she'd had to bet on what his home would look like, she would have won the bet. It was clean, tidy and had almost no personality. The neutral, comfortable furnishings looked as though they belonged in a model unit for showing prospective renters. There were very few knickknacks or artwork, and she would bet the few tasteful items he'd displayed had been gifts rather than chosen by him.

The bookshelves held a few battered paperbacks that looked to be all thrillers and mysteries. A big-screen TV sat on a simple wooden base. A magazine rack was stuffed with racing magazines.

He took her on a quick tour. The kitchen was neat and bright, with white cabinet fronts, tile counters and stainless-steel appliances. The dining room held a table and four chairs, with a simple arrangement of three candles in wrought-iron bases as a centerpiece. The room looked as though it had never been used.

His bedroom was as bland as the living room, though at least there were some grooming items available to show that someone did, indeed, live here. A tiny, second bedroom served as a home office; here, he had state-of-the-art computer equipment, stacks of papers and more racing magazines and a few pieces of team memorabilia. It was the only room in the apartment that showed a glimpse of who he really was.

A wooden deck was accessed by a sliding-glass door in the living room. The deck held a mountain bike locked to the wrought-iron railing, a little round patio table with two chairs and a small but efficient-looking gas grill. He turned on the grill to begin heating for their steaks.

"Your place is very nice," she told him, glancing over the railing at the wooded landscape beyond.

"Thanks," he said, motioning her back inside. "I've been told it's a little boring," he added with a wry smile.

She wondered who'd told him that. Family? Friends? Other women he'd brought home?

"It's not boring," she said, pushing that latter question to the back of her mind. "A little impersonal, maybe."

Much like his motor home. Tobey wasn't one to reveal much about himself, in his decor or his conversations.

They made comfortable small talk while they prepared the meal together. Even though he'd offered to cook, she would rather help than sit and wait, so she added a few ingredients to the prepackaged salad while he grilled the steaks to medium, as she'd requested. Mostly they talked about work, but since that was a topic that interested them both, she didn't mind.

They ate on the patio rather than in the spartan dining room. A nice breeze caressed their skin during the meal, making the neighbor's wind chimes play a merry tune as background music. Someone's dog barked a few times in the distance, and they could hear the muted sound of voices from somewhere nearby, but the deck was private enough to give the illusion that they were completely alone.

Dessert was a coconut cake Tobey had picked up at a nearby bakery. He served it with decaf coffee and even though she was full, Amy allowed herself one thin slice. Afterward, they cleaned the kitchen together, stacking their plates and cutlery in the dishwasher and putting the leftover salad and cake in the fridge.

"This was really nice," she said, draping a dishcloth over the side of the sink to dry. "I've enjoyed it."

"I'm glad. I know you have home-cooked meals all the time, but I get a little tired of restaurants."

"I can understand that. If I lived alone, I'd probably eat a lot of takeout and restaurant food myself. A home-cooked meal would be a treat."

"Exactly." He studied her face as she leaned back against the countertop. "I know you enjoy your family, but do you ever wish you had the chance to live alone? After all, you've been responsible for your sister almost your entire adult life."

"I don't regret taking responsibility for Gretchen, of course. But," she admitted slowly, "maybe there have been times when I wonder how my life would have been different if Mom and Dad hadn't died in that wreck. Maybe I could have pursued my career a little sooner, a little more aggressively. Maybe I'd have gotten a graduate degree and gone into upper management. Maybe I'd have opened my own public relations firm by now, without having to worry about the financial risk to my family if it wasn't immediately successful."

"You only talk about how your work life would have been different," he pointed out.

She laughed wryly. "Yeah. I guess I really am a hopeless workaholic. I rarely even think about how my life might be different off the job."

"Why do I have the feeling," he asked ironically, "that you would be living much the same way I do?"

"You're probably right. You and I do seem to be a lot alike."

Moving deliberately, he planted a hand on the counter on either side of her. "The thought has crossed my mind," he murmured, looking down at her smile.

The smile promptly faded as her pulse kicked into overdrive. This was the part of the evening she had been a little nervous about. And she'd known it was coming.

His eyelids lifted, so that their gazes met and held. He didn't say anything, but then he didn't have to. The question was written very clearly in his expression.

Holding her breath, she searched his face. Searched her own heart. And then leaned toward him, wrapping her arms around his neck and pressing her mouth to his.

For once, there was nowhere either of them needed to be for the next few hours.

CHAPTER THIRTEEN

EACH VENUE in racing had a distinct personality. The track in Dover, Delaware, was one of Amy's favorites. It was loud, dusty and chaotic, and it always reminded her of a big, freewheeling carnival. Souvenirs, food, games, rides. Every color of the rainbow. The smells of barbecues and beer, gas fumes and rubber, sweat and perfumes. Crazy—but she loved it. Or maybe it was just especially fun this particular weekend because she was so happy.

She and Tobey started the weekend with a slight disagreement. He wanted her to stay at his motor home rather than at the crowded hotel where the team rooms had been booked. "It would be so much more convenient for you," he'd argued. "Trust me, I know from experience how much time you save in commuting and how nice it is to stay so close to everything."

But convenience hadn't been enough to convince her. It was true that they had made no effort to hide their developing relationship, but she saw no reason to broadcast it, either. Not just yet. And there was no way the whole racing world wouldn't know if she stayed in Tobey's motor home.

She was a little surprised that Tobey *was* ready for that step. But when she said so, he merely shrugged and said everyone already knew, or at least suspected, anyway. Besides, he had added with just a bit of a pout, he wanted her there.

She had patted his cheek and told him he was sweet, but that she was keeping her hotel room. Later, she had wondered if she'd done so more out of self-protectiveness than to deter gossip. As long as she felt as though Tobey was holding back in this relationship, she didn't want to give too much of herself, either. It would be much easier if—when—the affair ended if she kept a part of her life separate from him.

Everything proceeded as usual after that. She and Kent did their typical rushing from one commitment to the next, sometimes joined by Tobey or Dawson, other times not. Tanya was there that weekend, too, but she hung out with her friends among the racing wives and girlfriends and with Kent's mother while Kent was otherwise occupied. When Kent was in the car, Amy was on the phone or the computer, making and taking calls, sending and responding to e-mail, dealing and scheduling and putting out fires. Tobey was in the garage most of the time, huddled with his team around the car, hunched over computers or reviewing tapes with the pit crew.

Whenever they found a few minutes free, Amy and Tobey slipped away to his motor home.

Anna hadn't come to Dover, so Amy had dinner Saturday evening with Dawson, Kent, Tanya and Tobey. They'd chosen a nice Italian restaurant where the food was excellent and the ambience subdued. They were able to get a quiet table in the back, no mean feat on this weekend when so many race fans had poured into the area.

The men talked about tires during appetizers. Tires were a big issue at Dover and races were won and lost there on tire wear. During the first course, the discussion centered around fuel efficiency and moved on from there to which line would be best for Kent to run, high or low.

Tanya and Amy carried on a separate conversation for the most part, speaking quietly to each other during the technical talk. It was as dessert was being served that Dawson winced and apologized. "I'm sorry, ladies. We've been pretty rude, haven't we? I'm sure neither of you are interested in hearing all this nuts-and-bolts talk."

"Both of us have heard it plenty of times before," Tanya answered with a laugh. "We even understand most of it. It's just that I, for one, have little to add to the topic."

"Me, either," Amy agreed. "Talk about promotion, and I'm in, but wedge and camber adjustments and fuel efficiency and such are just not my area of expertise."

"But please, talk about whatever you need to discuss," Tanya urged. "Amy and I have been having a perfectly lovely conversation."

"No. Let's all talk now," Dawson insisted. "Tell me how the wedding plans are going."

Kent groaned.

Giving him a look, Tanya replied, "They're going fine, thank you. Kent's just tired of being asked to make decisions."

"I keep asking Tanya to tell me when and where to show up and I'll be there, but she insists on asking my opinion about colors and flowers and music and food and stuff," Kent complained good-naturedly. "And then when I give a suggestion, she shoots it down."

Tanya rolled her eyes. "He suggested we use the team colors—red and blue. And that the groomsmen wear uniforms with their names embroidered on the back. He says someone could wave a green flag when we enter the church, a white flag when we say our vows and a checkered flag when the officiate pronounces us married."

"Hey, instead of rice, the guests could spray you both down with champagne as you run to the car. The race car, of course," Tobey teased.

"And just where would I sit in a race car?" Tanya demanded with feigned indignation. "There's only one seat."

"We could tie you to the hood," Kent suggested, earning himself a punch on the arm that left him muttering and rubbing the spot.

"I remember all the hoopla that went along with my wedding," Dawson announced, shaking his balding head as he dipped a spoon into his tiramisu. "Anna and her mother went sort of crazy, but I guess it turned out nice."

"Our wedding is going to be nice, too," Tanya assured them all, shaking a finger at Kent. "And there won't be any tying anyone to the hood of a car."

He laughed and glanced at Tobey. "See what you've missed by never getting engaged?"

Amy saw Tobey's expression change rapidly, the

laughter leaving his eyes as he murmured, "Actually, I was engaged once."

Everyone looked startled, but not as stunned as Amy felt. Tobey had been engaged? And he'd never thought to mention it to her, not even when she had told him about her serious relationship with Brandon before her parents died?

Tobey looked as though he was sorry he had mentioned it, and wasn't sure why he had. Maybe he'd just gotten caught up in the subject, or had responded without thinking to Kent's comment. He gave Amy a glance that might have held a hint of apology, as if he'd realized how badly he'd caught her off guard.

"You never mentioned that before," Kent said, speaking for all of them.

"Yes, well, it was a long time ago. Anyone besides me want more coffee?" He signaled for their server, making it clear that he'd like to change the subject. Everyone else went along, listening attentively as Dawson quickly began to tell a funny story about something Anna had done earlier that week.

Amy felt as though she had been punched in the stomach. She made a massive effort to keep her face pleasantly expressionless, but it wasn't easy. How could Tobey let her find out this way? They'd talked about her former boyfriend, and yet he'd never shared this significant event in his past. She'd always felt as though there was something he held back from her, but she'd had no idea it was anything like this.

He'd been engaged. As far as she was concerned, it

was a sign of how casually he thought of their present relationship that he'd never seen fit to talk about his former one.

He had never lied to her, she reminded herself, pretending to enjoy the last few bites of her Italian cream cake, though it might as well have been made of cotton, for all she could taste it. He'd told her straight from the beginning that he wasn't looking for long-term. He was attracted to her, he enjoyed being with her. He wasn't a monk, and he saw no need to live like one as long as she didn't want too much from him.

Looking at it from that standpoint, it was no big deal that he hadn't talked about his past. She'd thought she'd come to terms with it. Now she understood that she had only been fooling herself.

The dinner party broke up shortly afterward. Tobey drove Amy back to her hotel. The remark about his former engagement sat in the car between them like the proverbial elephant. Amy was the one who finally decided it was ridiculous not to acknowledge it. "So you were engaged?"

He cleared his throat. "Yeah. I guess I never mentioned that to you before."

"No." He knew very well that he hadn't.

"It didn't work out," he said in a tone that revealed little. "Jenny and I got engaged over Christmas during our junior year of college. Frankly, it was more her idea than mine, but I went along with it because I was crazy about her. I was very involved with racing even then, spending most of my weekends hanging out at the track, volunteering in the garages, filling in on pit crews whenever there was an opening, trying to talk my way into a permanent position. A lot like Josh does now."

She nodded, waiting for him to continue.

"I believe Jenny and her parents thought it was a phase I was going through, something I would outgrow. By the following year as we entered our final semester of college and I still had no interest in pursuing any job except this one, they realized the obsession wasn't going away. I was spending every spare minute at the tracks by that point, and Jenny felt neglected. She finally gave me an ultimatum—give up racing and find a less demanding career or end our engagement."

Knowing Tobey—and wondering how anyone could have expected differently from him—Amy said, "I guess we know what you chose."

His fingers flexed on the steering wheel. "Yeah. We broke it off. She was…pretty upset. I was, too, but I knew I'd never be happy in any other career and I certainly couldn't make Jenny happy if I was miserable myself."

"That makes sense," she replied, thinking of her own youthful, broken romance. She'd been unable to walk away from her responsibilities to her family. Just as she knew she wouldn't quit the job she loved now merely to please someone else.

Tobey's knuckles were white now from his grip on the wheel. "Jenny died in an accident six weeks after we broke up. She was killed when the car she was driving stalled on train tracks and she was hit by a train."

Shocked, Amy whispered, "Oh, Tobey. I'm so sorry."

He added in a dull, almost hoarse tone, "A week after the funeral, one of her friends told me Jenny had confided in her that she was pregnant. She was going to tell me the night she died. Her friend thought I should know—and she wasn't particularly kind about it."

This time, Amy simply didn't know what to say. She pressed a hand to her mouth, imagining how Tobey must have suffered during that time. And how the tragedy would have left him shocked and confused.

"Anyway, now you know," he said, trying a little too hard to speak lightly. "I've always been a hopeless workaholic. I guess I always will be."

Was that supposed to be a subtle warning that he still wasn't interested in a more serious relationship? In making commitments or talking about the future? Was he telling her, in case she'd wondered, that his one failed attempt at an engagement had put him off the idea of marriage forever?

"There's no need to walk me up," she said brightly when he parked in the hotel lot. "This is a perfectly safe hotel."

"Amy."

She was already reaching for the door handle. "Yes?"

He hesitated, then shook his head. "Never mind. I'll see you tomorrow."

"Of course." She moved again to open her door, but was stopped when he wrapped a hand around the back of her neck and tugged her to him for a kiss that almost steamed the windows in the car.

"Good night," he said when he finally released her.

Unable to trust her voice, she merely nodded and made her escape.

KENT CAME IN SECOND at Dover, putting him in second place in the Chase for the NASCAR Sprint Cup, only a few points behind his dad. Tobey could imagine the conflict that caused his driver. On the one hand, Kent would love to see his father win a championship, something that had eluded Dean in an otherwise very successful racing career. On the other hand, Kent was ambitious enough to want that trophy for himself. A way of proving that his first win hadn't been a fluke.

As for Tobey, as much as he respected Dean Grosso both as a decent man and as a legendary driver, he had no such conflict. He wanted that championship. For Kent. For himself.

He looked up from his desk late Tuesday afternoon to see Gretchen Barber standing in his doorway. Lifting his eyebrows in surprise, he smiled. "This is a surprise. What are you doing here?"

"I'm supposed to be waiting for Amy in the lobby, but I sneaked up here. I wanted to say hi."

"Come in. How's school going?"

She entered with a curious look around, making him aware that the office was still pretty cluttered. He'd had time to do very little in here since Neil had left, even though he kept meaning to do some straightening and rearranging. The way his schedule looked now, it would probably be after the season ended before he had a chance to get to that.

"It's okay," she said. "I hate my English teacher."

He chuckled. "Already?"

"Yeah. She's mean. Already gave us an essay to write, can you believe it?"

He shook his head in sympathy. "Unforgivable."

"Now you're teasing me," she said, leaning against the edge of his desk with a grin.

"Maybe a little. So you're supposed to meet Amy, huh?" He had seen little of Amy himself for the past couple of days.

She'd claimed it was an extremely busy week, and he believed her. This close to the end of the season, with Kent doing so well in points, plus the extra angle of battling with his own father for the points lead, Tobey had no doubt that the public relations machine was in full swing. Heck, he was crazy busy this week getting ready for the Kansas race, making sure everything was on schedule.

Gretchen nodded. "Tonight's open house at school. The night when parents are supposed to meet all the teachers and stuff. The choir's singing the National Anthem at the opening assembly. I sing second soprano. We've been practicing all week."

"I'm sure you'll do a great job."

"Why don't you come with us and hear for yourself?"

"Um…come with you? To your open house?"

"Sure. All the families are invited. There will be cookies and punch," she added enticingly.

Families. He gave her a strained smile and said, "Thanks for the invitation, Gretchen, but I really can't tonight. I'm snowed under."

"Oh." She looked disappointed, but she didn't try to

change his mind. He figured watching her sister had taught her plenty about the demands of work. "Okay."

"Maybe I'll hear you sing some other time," he said, fighting a ripple of guilt.

"We'll be doing a big Christmas concert," she said eagerly. "We've already started practicing. Maybe you'll come to that?"

Christmas. Still several months away. He didn't commit that far ahead. The fewer promises he made, the fewer people he would disappoint.

Fortunately, before he had to say anything, Amy spoke from the doorway. "There you are. I thought I told you to wait for me downstairs while I took that call, Gretchen. I didn't say you could come up and bother Tobey."

"She isn't bothering me," Tobey replied before Gretchen could attempt to defend herself. "It's always a pleasure to see Gretchen."

Gretchen gave her sister a rather smug look, and Tobey wondered if he should have said anything. He didn't want to contribute to the girl's rebelliousness.

"We'd better go," Amy said to Gretchen. "If we're late, your choir teacher will be annoyed."

"Okay. Bye, Tobey. Maybe next time, okay?"

"Yeah," he said. "Maybe."

Amy looked a bit questioning, but apparently didn't have time to stay and ask. "See you tomorrow, Tobey."

He looked at the faint lines of stress around her mouth and wished he had the opportunity to kiss them away. "See you tomorrow."

He stared at the empty doorway for several long

minutes after the sisters left. And then he reached into his desk drawer for the roll of antacids he hadn't needed in a while.

KANSAS WAS A track known for giving the fans a great deal of access to the drivers and teams. A "fan walk" allowed spectators to watch the crew chiefs and team members huddle over the cars in the garages and to gawk as the pits were set up. They were able to watch prerace car inspections and beg attention from drivers who passed by a fence lined with openings through which fans could hand over items to be autographed. That interaction of fans and drivers was one of the treasured hallmarks of stock car racing.

Amy made sure Kent was very visible at the track. Race results were important, of course, but popularity helped sell sponsorships as much as statistics.

Tobey was busy. *Very* busy. So busy that she barely saw him. And she didn't for a minute believe that it wasn't deliberate, since she had been avoiding him, too. She couldn't be too annoyed with him. But when his behaviour started interfering with her work, she knew she had to do something about it.

He must have seen her number on the ID screen of his phone Saturday afternoon. He answered with only barely concealed impatience. "H'lo."

"I thought we were going to have a meeting this afternoon about the sports network interview," she said without bothering with preliminaries. "If we don't get together soon, it's going to be too late."

"Look, Amy, I really don't have time now. I'm in the garage and we've got some issues here."

"I know you're busy, but your interview is in less than two hours. You said you wanted to go over some things with me first."

"I know, but I just don't think I'm going to have time. I'll just wing it."

"Are you sure?" she asked with a frown. "Because it would only take about fifteen minutes for us to go over my notes."

"I don't have fifteen minutes. It'll be okay."

"Fine. Just try not to be late, because the—"

"Look, I know how to do my job, okay? I said I'll handle it."

"Fine," she said again, hearing the ice in her tone now. "I'll see you later."

"Yeah. Sure. Later."

Muttering beneath her breath, Amy snapped her phone closed.

Kent skidded to a stop as he approached her, his expression suddenly wary. "Don't tell me you're in a bad mood, too?"

She smoothed her frown. "No, I'm not in a bad mood."

"Good. Because Tobey's pretty much a bear this weekend. Of course, there are a lot of problems in the garage, but still."

She nodded, keeping her own expression determinedly pleasant. "I've noticed. So, are you ready for the photo shoot?"

"As ready as I'm going to be," he said with a small

groan that made her smile, as he intended. Neither of them mentioned Tobey again, though Amy wondered if she detected a certain amount of speculation in Kent's eyes as he studied her.

Tobey left a message on her voice mail later that he didn't have time to take off for dinner. She politely declined Kent's invitation to have dinner with Tanya and him, choosing, instead, to join some other reps from MMG for dinner. It had been ages since she, Anita and Kylie had a chance to get together and compare notes, both business and personal. She didn't mention Tobey, other than to say the new command structure was working out well.

After a rather restless night, she saw Tobey again the next morning. He greeted her pleasantly enough, though his gaze didn't quite meet hers. They were surrounded by people all morning as the race drew near. Lucky fans with pit passes wandered through the area up to an hour before the race began, and the teams were under close scrutiny. Despite the grumpy mood he'd been in earlier that weekend, Tobey seemed to make an effort to be friendly and positive in front of the spectators.

Amy fully intended to have a talk with Tobey, but she would wait until after the race, she decided. That was, after all, the number-one priority this weekend, just as it always was with them. The job came first—even if she was ticked off with him.

Kent finished the Kansas race with the fifth fastest time. Justin Murphy won—to Kent's sister's pleasure and Kent's disgust.

The win moved Justin up from fifth to fourth in points. Kent's position remained unchanged. Unfortunately, Dean had a horrible race and lost several points positions. Amy saw the disappointment in Kent's expression and suspected he was thinking that setback would not ease the tension in his parents' home.

Maybe Tobey was right, she thought wearily, packing up to head home. Maybe racing and relationships were too difficult to combine. Some could pull it off, but for too many people, it was just too hard.

She was weary and discouraged when she walked into her house that evening, but she had no intention of letting her family see those feelings. She greeted her great-aunt with a kiss on the cheek, and her sister with a hug.

"I brought you something," she added to Gretchen, handing her a bag. "Don't expect a gift from every venue," she added with a slight laugh, "but I saw this in the window of a little shop close to my hotel and I thought you'd like it."

Gretchen pulled the green-and-white-striped hoodie sweater from the bag and smiled. "It's pretty. Thanks, Amy."

She seemed to really like the sweater, and to be grateful for it—but Amy couldn't help thinking that Gretchen had been much more excited about the gift from Tobey. "It'll be a few weeks before the weather's cool enough for you to wear it, but winter will be here before we know it."

Something about that sentiment made her a little sad.

Maybe because she was pretty sure that by the time winter arrived, she and Tobey would be no more than polite co-workers.

"Is Tobey coming over for dinner this week?" Gretchen wanted to know. She'd been disappointed that she hadn't seen him in a couple of weeks, though Amy had made excuses that he was very busy.

"I don't know, Gretchen. It's hard for Tobey to get much time away this late in the season."

Gretchen was perhaps a bit more perceptive than Amy gave her credit for at times. She gave her a sharp look. "Is everything okay with you and Tobey?"

"Everything's fine," she said brightly, aware that her great-aunt was also looking at her a bit closely. "We're still really good friends."

Gretchen frowned. Aunt Ellen swiftly stepped in. "You look tired, Amy. Would you like some hot tea?"

Amy nodded gratefully. "I would love some. Thank you."

She hoped Gretchen had finally gotten the message that there wasn't going to be a happily-ever-after romance for Amy and Tobey, despite Gretchen's romanticized fantasies. Their family was just fine the way they were, and Amy wanted Gretchen to understand that, since it didn't look as though anything was going to be changing in the near future.

AMY FINALLY LOST her temper on Tuesday.

She'd been trying to track Tobey down all day, leaving messages he hadn't returned, even sending him an e-mail. She knew how hard he was working to get ready for Talladega that weekend, but she'd had enough.

She cornered him in his office just before 6:00 p.m. Without waiting to be invited, she walked in and all but slammed the door closed behind her. She was glad most of the other office staff had already left for the day. It was entirely possible that voices were about to be raised.

Tobey looked up, startled. "Amy? What—?"

"I have been trying to reach you all day. Don't tell me you didn't know it."

Immediately on the defensive, he said, "I've been busy."

She slammed both hands down on the desk and leaned forward so that she glared directly into his eyes. "We're all busy, Harris. But because you didn't bother to return my calls or answer my e-mail, my job today was made much more difficult. I needed an answer from you by five o'clock. Because I didn't get it, we lost a damned good promotional opportunity for both you and the team."

He looked rather stunned by the ferocity of her tone, but she didn't give him a chance to make any more feeble excuses. "I was not trying to reach you to chitchat. I didn't want to have lunch or see a movie or sneak away for a little afternoon delight. *You're* the one who said you didn't want anything personal between us to inter-fere with the job, but you're the one who's doing just that with this silly avoidance game you've been playing. When I try to reach you at work, it's *for* work. Is that clear?"

"Look, I didn't—"

"You didn't think I was trying to track you down in hopes of getting your attention?" she demanded.

"I, uh—"

"Yeah, that's just what I thought," she said in open disgust.

He shook his head with a quick frown. "That isn't it. I just got tied up with other stuff. I was going to call you back, but I thought it could wait. I didn't know you had a five o'clock deadline."

"Because you didn't give me a chance to tell you." She straightened and leveled a finger at him. "Let me make this easy for you, Tobey. The thing between you and me? It's over. When I call you—which I will, because that's my job—it will be for business purposes. I'll expect you to respond. We will continue to have team dinners together, I'll be just as diligent as ever in prepping you for the media, and we will smile and chat politely whenever our paths cross on the job, because that's what we do. Clear?"

"Amy—"

She was already moving toward the door. "I'll let you get back to work. Because I know how *busy* you are."

She paused at the door, then turned slowly to look at him, just a hint of sadness ripping through her. "And by the way? I've lost people, too, Tobey. It hurt. But I didn't let it stop me from living."

She closed the door behind her on the way out.

CHAPTER FOURTEEN

TOBEY, KENT, Joey and Steve huddled over a computer in Tobey's office late on the afternoon before they were to leave for the track. Every note, every statistic, every detail of the previous Talladega race was under last-minute scrutiny. So much was riding on this weekend, points-wise. The superspeedways were always a challenge with forty-three drivers doing everything they could to avoid being caught up in a multicar accident.

Tobey was focused completely on the job. Of course he was, he thought firmly. Nothing was more important to him than this, he assured himself.

Not anymore.

It amazed even him that he could be so calm, cool and collected on the job when he'd had maybe an hour's restless sleep the night before. He still felt as though someone had reached into his chest and ripped the heart right out of him, leaving him aching, defeated—and so very much alone.

It wasn't the first time, he reminded himself, nodding somberly as Joey pointed to a row of numbers. But it would be the last. He would never put himself in a position to be hurt that way again. He should have known better this time.

He always found a way to mess it up.

"Don't you agree, Tobey?" Kent asked.

"Absolutely." And the thing was, he knew exactly what he was agreeing to. Because, despite the anguish he'd been feeling since Amy had glared into his eyes and told him it was over between them, he was still able to do his job.

He glanced up at the open doorway, realizing that someone was hovering there. For just a moment, he thought it might be Amy, and his chest tightened. When he realized it was Linda from downstairs, he relaxed and told himself he was relieved.

"Do you need something, Linda?" he asked.

She moistened her lips. "I, um, thought there's something you guys should know. It's about Amy. Well, her little sister, really."

Tobey's whole body went rigid in response to that. He pushed himself away from the desk, taking a step toward the receptionist. "Something's happened to Gretchen?"

"I don't know. Amy got a call, and she ran out in a panic about ten minutes ago. She told me to cancel her appointment this afternoon and when I asked why, she said she had to go find her little sister. She said she was missing."

Missing. The word slammed into him with the force of a bullet.

Without hesitation, he turned to the other men. "I have to—"

"Go!" Kent said immediately. "Call me when you find out what's going on. Let me know if there's anything I can—"

Tobey was running for the parking lot before Kent could even finish the sentence.

TOBEY BRAKED in Amy's driveway and threw his car into Park, jumping out of the seat almost before the engine died. He reached the front door just as Amy was coming out.

Her face was white, he noted immediately. Her hair was tousled, and her hands were unsteady. She stared up at him for a moment almost as if she didn't recognize him. And then she gripped his arm. "Did she call you?"

"No." He covered her icy hand with his, feeling her fear wash into him. "What happened?"

"She didn't come home from school. She should have been here two hours ago, but she never showed up."

"You called her friends?"

"Yes. They all say they haven't seen her."

"Where are you going?"

"I—" She looked down at the keys in her hand as if trying to remember. "I was just going to drive the route from here to the school. I just…I have to do something."

"Come back in the house. Let's talk about what we should do."

Aunt Ellen was pacing in the living room when he coaxed Amy back into the house. "Oh, Tobey, thank God you're here," she said, her face pale and strained. "We're going crazy."

"Can you tell me what happened?"

"She was angry when she left this morning," Ellen admitted. "Amy and I grounded her for the rest of the week because she's been defying us again, talking on the telephone after she was supposed to be in bed Monday night, not doing her homework yesterday when she said she had. Just generally acting out. And then she didn't come home from school."

"Did you call the police?"

"I did," Aunt Ellen said. "They said they would look for her, but they seem to think she's just sulking at one of her friend's houses."

"You're absolutely sure she's not?"

"We're not absolutely sure about anything at this point," Amy replied, her arms crossed tightly in front of her. "But I called everyone I could think of, and they all denied knowing where she is."

"Well, they would, wouldn't they, if she'd asked them to?"

"Probably," she agreed, her shoulders sagging.

He tried to rein in his own fear enough to think clearly. "Who's her best friend?"

Amy answered again. "Either Jessica or Emily. I called them both. They said they didn't know where she was."

"Did you call that boy? The one she likes to play video games with?"

"I called. No one answered at his house."

"Really." He thought about that a moment, then said, "Can you tell me his address? I'll go check it out."

Amy nodded. "I'll go with you."

He waited until she'd followed him onto the front porch before saying, "Maybe you should stay here with your aunt. She looks pretty upset. And you should probably be here in case Gretchen or the police call."

Looking torn, Amy glanced from his car to the front door. "But I—"

"I'll go look for her, Amy. Just tell me her friends' addresses. You stay here and keep making calls. I'm really worried about your aunt being alone when she's so upset."

She sighed and capitulated, swayed by his argument. "Okay. I'll be right back."

She was gone only a couple of minutes, returning with a slip of paper with several address scribbled on it. "Carson's is the first one," she said, unnecessarily since she'd written names beside the addresses.

"I'll try there first."

"You'll call me if…?"

He gave her arm a bracing squeeze. "Yeah. And you call me if you hear anything."

"I will." She gazed up at him with damp eyes and whispered, "Thank you, Tobey."

Unable to reply, he merely nodded and turned toward his car.

He drove straight to the boy's house, some instinct telling him that should be his first stop. The brick-and-siding house sat in a middle-class neighborhood only a few blocks from Amy's home. There were no cars in the driveway, but he saw a curtain twitch when he stepped onto the front porch.

Hoping it wasn't premature, he felt a wave of relief go through him. Somehow he knew Gretchen was inside this house. With a hand that wasn't quite steady, he knocked on the door.

No one answered, but he saw the curtain twitch again.

Taking a gamble, he spoke loudly through the wooden door. "Gretchen, I know you're in there. It's Tobey. Open the door. I need to know you're okay."

After a pause during which he counted slowly to five, the door opened. Red-faced and swollen-eyed, Gretchen faced him sullenly.

His first reaction was to grab her and pull her into his arms. His second was to turn her over his knee. But all he did was exhale slowly and whisper, "Thank God."

"How did you know I was here?" she demanded.

"Call it a hunch. Where's the boy?"

A skinny, emo-haired kid with black-rimmed glasses and nervous blue eyes stepped behind Gretchen. "I told her she needed to call home, but she didn't want to. My parents will be home in a few minutes, and I figured my mom could talk to her," he said, sounding defensive.

Tobey raked Gretchen's coconspirator with a look that had the boy taking a nervous step backward, then said shortly, "That won't be necessary. Come on, Gretchen, I'm taking you home. Your aunt and your sister are worried sick about you."

"Like *you* care," Gretchen muttered.

Planting his fists on his hips, he asked, "What is that supposed to mean?"

"All you care about is your job. It's more important to

you than anything else. You're just like Amy. All she does is work. Neither one of you cares about anything else."

"I'm here, aren't I?" he asked evenly. "I walked right out of a meeting when I heard you were missing. A meeting that was pretty important, considering we're leaving for Talladega in the morning."

That information made her bite her lip in uncertainty before asking quietly, "You did that for me?"

"I did. And Amy canceled a very important meeting of her own to run home to look for you. She's waiting there now, taking care of Aunt Ellen while praying you'll call or come home. So let's go."

With a quick goodbye to her friend, Gretchen climbed into the passenger seat of Tobey's car, gripping her hands in her lap.

"Do your seat belt," he said, after fastening his own and starting the engine. He thought about calling Amy, but he could have Gretchen home almost as quickly as he could dial the number. He backed out of the driveway.

"I guess I'm going to be grounded for a month," she muttered, looking gloomily out the passenger window.

"If it were up to me, it would probably be even longer," he said without sympathy, remembering the sick look of worry on her great-aunt's lined face. "Aunt Ellen didn't deserve to be treated that way. Neither did Amy."

"Amy would probably be glad if I didn't come home at all," Gretchen stated. "All I do is get in her way."

Tobey pulled his gaze away from the road long enough to give the girl a quick, incredulous look. "What on earth are you talking about?"

"All she wants to do is work. And even when she isn't working, I hold her back."

"That's just nuts, Gretchen," he said flatly. "Amy doesn't see you as a burden at all. She loves you."

But Gretchen was immersed in full teen-tragedy mode now, he realized, when she said, "She'd be better off if I wasn't around."

He shook his head. "You're wrong about that. Amy loves you. She's very glad to have you in her life."

"What life? She's got work, and she's got me and Aunt Ellen. If it weren't for us, she could be having fun."

"Amy is very happy with her life. She loves her job and she loves her family. She lives exactly the way she wants to."

"Like she has any other choice."

He turned onto the street where she lived. "She has plenty of choices."

Gretchen grew visibly more tense as they approached her house. "You don't care. You weren't planning to come back, anyway."

He sighed. It had been a long time since he'd had to deal with adolescent drama. Remembering some of the tearful hissy fits his sisters had thrown in their early teens, he tried to stay patient. "Now what are you talking about?"

"I heard Amy tell Aunt Ellen that you wouldn't be coming back to our house anymore. You think I don't know it's because of me?"

Pulling into her driveway, he said firmly as he put the car into Park, "It is not because of you."

"Come on, Tobey. Be honest with me. You're not the first guy who took off because of me and Aunt Ellen."

"I want you to get this straight, Gretchen. You and Aunt Ellen have nothing to do with anything that has happened between Amy and me," he said as decisively as he could manage. "*Nothing.* Now, go in the house and let your family know that you're safe and that you're very sorry you hurt them. I've got to make a call to let Kent and the other guys know you're okay before they call out the National Guard to look for you, and then I'll be in."

Her shoulders drooping, she opened her door.

"Gretchen."

She looked around at him, obviously expecting another scolding. "What?"

He looped a hand around the back of her neck, looking into her teary eyes. "We all mess up, kiddo. We all do stupid things. I did more than my share when I was your age. You're a very special girl, and I know your sister loves you and that she's very proud of you. If her rules seem a little strict to you sometimes, it's only because she loves you so much and she wants so badly to keep you safe. Cut her a little slack, okay?"

She sniffled and nodded.

Brushing a kiss against the top of her head, he released her. "All right, go on in. And don't bother with all the excuses and drama, okay? Just tell them you're sorry and you'll try not to scare them like that again."

Nodding again, she climbed out of the car and headed for the front door.

He'd probably wasted his breath with the advice about not trying to defend her actions, he figured. He doubted that Gretchen would be able to resist a few self-pitying monologues.

Pulling out his phone, he dialed Kent's number. Kent answered on the first ring. "Tobey, I've been waiting to hear from you. Has Gretchen been found? Do I need to come there?"

"Gretchen's fine. She's home." Tobey saw no need to mention that he'd been the one to find her. "She'd gone to a friend's house to sulk about being grounded for a week."

Relief was audible in Kent's short laugh. "She's probably going to be grounded for a year now."

"Yeah, maybe. Listen, Kent, about my running out on you earlier…"

"You hardly ran out on me. I didn't blame you a bit for leaving to help Amy. I was tempted to go with you."

Tobey appreciated the support, but felt obligated to say, "I just don't want you to think I'm going to fall into the same trap Neil did. I'm not going to let my personal life interfere with the job. It was just, when I heard Gretchen was missing, I—"

"Tobey, come on," Kent interrupted with just a hint of impatience. "The problem with Neil was that he started to let *everything* take precedence over the job. You've been nothing but professional from day one. But I would seriously question your priorities if you just kept running numbers after hearing that your girlfriend's little sister had gone missing."

"My...uh...girlfriend?"

Kent laughed again, a little sheepishly this time. "Okay, I know you've had a quarrel. You've been as snappy as a badger and Amy's chin goes up about two inches every time you come into the vicinity. Anyone with half a brain can put two and two together and figure out you're mad at each other. But anyone with a whole brain can tell just by looking at the two of you that you're crazy about each other. Tanya and I have done our share of bickering. You'll work it out—we always have."

Tobey cleared his throat. "Yes, well—"

"Sorry," Kent cut in again. "Now who's getting too personal? I know this is none of my business, chief. You just take care of things there, and I'll see you when you get back."

Tobey closed his phone thoughtfully, considering Kent's confidence that Tobey and Amy would be together. Kent seemed to believe it had been nothing more than a lover's spat that had driven them apart. Tobey wondered what the intrepid driver would think if he learned that their problems were based on pure fear instead. Mostly on Tobey's part.

The passenger door of the car opened and Amy slid into the seat Gretchen had vacated only minutes earlier. "I wanted to thank you in private," she said. "I can't tell you how much I appreciate your bringing Gretchen home."

Tobey turned in his seat to look at her. She was still a bit pale from the ordeal, but she'd gotten herself fully under control now. "Is your aunt okay?"

Tucking a strand of hair behind her ear, she nodded. "She's fine. Now. Thank you, Tobey."

"You would have found her yourself. I just wanted to do what I could to help."

"Whatever you said to her on the way here must have had an effect. She told us both she was sorry and said she had no excuses for what she did—though she couldn't resist adding that she still wishes we wouldn't treat her like a child. She said she would accept whatever punishment we thought was fair."

A little surprised that Gretchen had taken his advice—and a bit suspicious that she thought her mature attitude would soften her sister and great-aunt enough to lessen that inevitable punishment—Tobey shrugged. "I simply told her how thoughtless she'd been. Told her how worried you and Aunt Ellen were about her. How worried we all were."

Amy studied his face. "How did you find out she was missing?"

"Linda came to my office and interrupted a meeting between Kent, Joey, Steve and me. Scared us all half to death when she said you'd rushed out to look for Gretchen."

"And you came to help us look for her."

He nodded. "Kent was just waiting for me to call and he'd have come to search, too. They all would have helped, you know. Everyone's fond of Gretchen."

"But you were the one who left the meeting and ran to help."

He squeezed the taut back of his neck with one hand.

"How could I think about work when I knew Gretchen was missing? When I knew how worried you must be?"

Knowing it was time to stop hiding his true feelings, from Amy and from himself, he said, "I've spent the past few weeks trying to convince myself that my job still took precedence over everything else in my life, but I've been lying to myself, Amy. Lying to both of us. I love my job. To the point of obsession, in most people's opinion. But, as it turns out, I love you every bit as much. I know that doesn't sound very romantic, but the thing is—I've never loved anyone else like this before. I never even knew I could."

STUDYING THE earnestness in Tobey's blue eyes, Amy swallowed hard. She wasn't going to cry, she assured herself. She'd cried enough over Tobey, though she had no intention of telling him so.

"Amy?" He searched her expression, apparently unable to read her expression. "Am I completely off track here? I know I've made a mess of things between us, but I thought—I hoped—"

Stopping himself impatiently, he shook his head. "I'm sorry. You're probably not in any mood to hear this right now, when you're still so shaken up by Gretchen. It's okay. I can wait."

He leaned a little closer to her, a determined look firming his attractive mouth. "I'm going to do everything I can to prove to you that we can make this work. That I've got enough to give to both you and to the job. And to Gretchen and Aunt Ellen, for that matter. We can be a family, Amy. It won't be easy, we both know that, but apparently, I thrive on challenge. I know you feel the same way, if you'll only forgive me enough to admit it."

When she still didn't speak, he glanced around as if suddenly becoming aware of their surroundings. "Damn it. I didn't mean to do this in my car. I don't blame you for being blindsided. We can—"

"Actually, it's probably appropriate that we're having this discussion in a car," she broke in, finally taking pity on him. But she couldn't say she hadn't enjoyed watching him fumble and squirm a little. She'd deserved that after what he'd put her through the past couple of weeks.

"I don't know what you mean," he said warily.

Her smile felt a bit unsteady. "Well, considering that the majority of our foreseeable future together is going to be spent in cars and airplanes and motor homes and other forms of transportation, a car seems like the logical place for me to tell you that I love you, too."

It took him about half a second to catch up. His eyes lighting, he reached for her. "Amy—"

She put a hand on his chest to hold him away. "You're the one who said this isn't going to be easy, and you're right. It's going to get crazy at times. I get too caught up in details and I don't always have enough patience to be tactful or tiptoe around sensitive ego areas. You have a tendency to snarl under stress, and I'm not always going to let you get away with that. Gretchen and Aunt

Ellen will have a home with me for as long as they need it, and there's nothing I can or would do to change that."

"I'm aware of all of the above," he assured her. "We'll work it out. And, by the way, I wouldn't change your family circumstances, either. I'm crazy about them both. Even your hormonal, adolescent sister. Your aunt's cooking alone is enough to make up for the difficulties."

She almost smiled at that, as he'd intended, but she kept her expression serious long enough to add in a low voice, "I don't want them hurt, Tobey. Be very sure."

His smile was tender enough to make her heart ache. "I'm sure," he said. "Do you know how terrified I was about Gretchen today? How worried I was about Aunt Ellen when she looked so frightened and upset?"

He shook his head, looking as though he was trying not to remember those moments too clearly. "As you reminded me so pointedly before, you know all too well how much it hurts to lose people you care about. How it leaves you afraid to get too close to anyone again for fear of reliving that agony. There's a good reason loved ones have been called 'hostages to fortune.' But as you also said so eloquently, I can't let fear stop me from living. From loving. And I won't let it stop me any longer."

"You think I wasn't scared spitless when I realized I was falling in love with you?" she asked with a shaky laugh. "I knew how daunting my family situation is for anyone. I knew how hard it will be to combine our crazy schedules. I knew how much risk we were both taking by trying to have a relationship with someone so integrally involved in our careers. But I fell, anyway. Hard. I just refused to be the only one willing to put myself out there."

"You made that clear," he said with a slight grimace. "I don't think there's any danger that you'll let me get away with ignoring my obligations outside the job for too long. And I'll try to make sure that you don't get too wrapped up in work to appreciate the rest of your life, either."

"It won't be easy," she felt the need to say one more time.

"You know what I said when Dawson offered me the crew chief's position? When he warned me that it was going to be tough stepping into Neil's shoes so late in the season? That it would be hard to gain everyone's trust, and prove I was the right man for the job?"

She shook her head with a quizzical smile. "No. What did you say?"

Pushing aside her hand so that he could gather her into his arms—at least the best he could considering the console between them—he smiled down at her. "I said, bring it on. Those challenges you've outlined for us? Bring them on, Amy. You've picked the right man for the job."

Her happy, thoroughly approving laugh was smothered beneath his kiss.

* * * * *

For more thrill-a-minute romances
set against the exciting backdrop of
the NASCAR world, don't miss:

RUNNING ON EMPTY by Ken Casper
Available in November

For a sneak peek, just turn the page!

"WHY DID YOU LEAVE?"

Sylvie went through the motions of taking a sip of her tea, but her stomach was too upset for her to do more than wet her lips. She'd been dreading this meeting, done her best to avoid it. Yet it seemed to her she'd been trying to prepare for it since the day she'd packed a few meager belongings in a tiny knapsack, kissed her napping daughter goodbye and slipped out the back door, while the babysitter watched TV in the front room.

"I had no choice, Hugo," she answered defiantly. "Staying would have been worse."

He gaped at her, brows knitted. He wasn't satisfied with the answer. She couldn't expect him to be, not without further explanation, and she knew he would get it. He'd always been dogged. It was one of the things that she'd admired about him, his quiet, nonthreatening but unrelenting persistence. Clearly he hadn't changed. He wouldn't be here now, after all these years, if he was one to give up, to let things go.

Their first meeting was still clear in her memory. She hadn't made many sales that day, though there had been plenty of foot traffic, and she was worried her boss might fire her. Hugo had passed by once, taken a brief glance at her and moved on, good-looking and a little cocky in his team uniform. Then he passed by again. This time he smiled at her. She had all she could do not to smile back. She had no intention of encouraging him or any other man. A few guys had made overtures, some less subtly than others, but she'd learned how to say no so that they understood it.

Hugo was different. She wasn't sure why, except that when he smiled at her he didn't make her feel like prey. It was a different sensation, as if he appreciated her for herself, not as an object or a means to something else, but as a person. That was a new experience for her.

Observing him now, after thirty years, she realized his looks hadn't changed—not much, anyway. His face no longer had the fresh glow of a teenager. The cockiness had been superseded by maturity. The thick dark hair of his youth was cut shorter now, and there was a distinguished sprinkling of gray at the temples. The man of fifty was even more attractive than the boy of nineteen. Subtle worry lines etched the corners of his eyes, but their hazel-green was as intense as it had been back then.

The next minutes and hours were going to be difficult for both of them. When it was over he would hate her even more than he had when she walked away, yet she still felt safe with him. No other man had ever made her feel the way Hugo Murphy had. He would hate her from the depths of his being in a little while, but he would never hurt her.

She'd made a terrible choice leaving him, leaving Kim, but she knew now more than ever, standing so close to him, that it had been the right decision.

The question was whether he could ever forgive her.

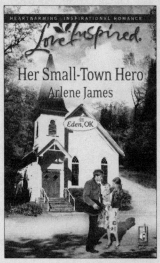

REQUEST YOUR FREE BOOKS!

2 FREE NOVELS PLUS 2 FREE GIFTS!

SPECIAL EDITION®

Life, Love and Family!